"Do you have any idea what you do to me, Sean?" Dalton murmured huskily. "Do you know how crazy you've been driving me these past twenty-four hours? Do you know how much I want to touch you? How much I want to kiss you?"

He stroked her cheek with his fingertips, sending hundreds of white-hot shivers shooting down her spine that felt as though they would likely melt her soul with their intensity.

"I . . . oh, I think I've got a good idea," she told him.

After all, she'd been feeling all of those same things about him.

He brushed his lips against her cheek again.

"But I also think it'd be even crazier if we allowed ourselves to act upon any of those impulses," she added.

His response was to tighten his grip on her hand and pull her closer until she was pressed against his body.

"Probably. Thing is, sweetheart," he said, "I guess I just don't care anymore . . . 'cause all I can think about is how much I want to kiss you right now."

Then he tilted her chin up and captured her mouth in a kiss unlike any other she'd known before. She surrendered to him, letting herself get lost in the power and the beauty of the kiss. It was all things wonderful . . . and all things most terrifying.

WHAT ARE *LOVESWEPT* ROMANCES?

They are stories of true romance and touching emotion. We believe those two very important ingredients are constants in our highly sensual and very believable stories in the LOVESWEPT line. Our goal is to give you, the reader, stories of consistently high quality that may sometimes make you laugh, sometimes make you cry, but are always fresh and creative and contain many delightful surprises within their pages.

Most romance fans read an enormous number of books. Those they truly love, they keep. Others may be traded with friends and soon forgotten. We hope that each LOVESWEPT romance will be a treasure—a "keeper." We will always try to publish

LOVE STORIES YOU'LL NEVER FORGET
BY AUTHORS YOU'LL ALWAYS REMEMBER

The Editors

Loveswept ®851

AFTERGLOW

FAYE
HUGHES

BANTAM BOOKS
NEW YORK · TORONTO · LONDON · SYDNEY · AUCKLAND

AFTERGLOW

A Bantam Book / September 1997

ISBN 0-553-44592-8

Published simultaneously in the United States and Canada

*Bantam Books are published by Bantam Books, a division of Bantam Dou-
bleday Dell Publishing Group, Inc. Its trademark, consisting of the words
"Bantam Books" and the portrayal of a rooster, is Registered in U.S.
Patent and Trademark Office and in other countries. Marca Registrada.
Bantam Books, 1540 Broadway, New York, New York 10036.*

PRINTED IN THE UNITED STATES OF AMERICA

OPM   10 9 8 7 6 5 4 3 2 1

This one is for Jeff. . . .

PROLOGUE

It rained the day of her daddy's funeral.

Not a light drizzle, either, but heavy sheets of water that fell so fast and hard, they threatened to turn the streets of Plaquemine, Louisiana, into a river. Ten-year-old Sean Kilpatrick wouldn't have minded all that much if they had. Floating down a river to the Gulf of Mexico and beyond would've suited her just fine. But the rain didn't make a river. It didn't even make a good-sized stream.

So Sean had done the next best thing.

When the grown-ups went inside her parents' five-room shotgun house after the church services to talk things through, she grabbed her eight-year-old brother Ian's hand and bolted out the back door to head for their tree house.

She had heard enough before the funeral

to know what the grown-ups were likely gonna say after it. There would be more of her mama's wailing and her uncle Hop's red-faced yelling about how he couldn't understand why Daddy could've gone and done what he did. Sean figured that hearing more of it would only make her head hurt and her stomach ache. Then there was Aunt Dale, always patting her arm and asking her if she was gonna cry.

Stupid question, Sean thought, scowling. She never cried. *Never.*

Sean shook out the water from her ponytail and glanced over at her brother. He had laid out his toy soldiers in a corner of the tree house and was beginning to play. She settled in to her own corner across from his and pulled her knees up to her chin. Then she started to read her most prized possession, a book about pirates that she'd traded Bobby Fontenot her favorite fishing pole for the week before.

It was quiet for a long time, except for the pelting of the rain against the tin roof.

"Sis?"

She glanced at Ian over the top of her book.

His face was all pale and drawn up as though a chigger had bit him good. The only spots of color were his wavy red hair and sad blue eyes.

"Is it true?" he whispered. "Is Mama really gonna send us to live with Uncle Hop and Aunt Dale over in Tall'hassee?"

She swallowed. "Just for a little while," she whispered back, and closed her book. "Maybe a week or two, Aunt Dale said."

Sean had a feeling it would be for a lot longer but didn't say so.

He stuck out his bottom lip. "I don't wanna go! Why can't we just stay here?"

She frowned. " 'Cause we can't, that's why. Look, Mudbug, Daddy's gone."

She had used the name she'd called him ever since he was a baby and had pinched her finger the way a crawdad would when you poked at it.

"Things . . . well, things are hard for Mama right now," she said. "You know."

Things had been hard for Mama for a long time—ever since Daddy had lost his job out on the oil rig and had taken to sitting by himself in his old Ford pickup, drinking his beer and staring into space. Sean had heard some people say that he and Mama should've never had kids 'cause they weren't cut out for the responsibilities.

Sometimes Sean had thought so too.

Ian's bottom lip started to shake, but she knew he wouldn't cry. He never did either.

"It'll be okay," she said. "Long as we're together. You and me's family, and ain't nobody ever gonna split us up. *Nobody*." She grinned. " 'Sides, Florida's got a lot of great spots to dig for pirate treasure. We're gonna strike it rich!"

"Yeah?"

"Shoot, yeah! Florida's where Jackson La-Rue spent most of his time, and he was a better pirate than ol' Jean Lafite. Why, LaRue had a treasure so big, it took ten men to carry it when he buried it."

She thumped the cover of her book. "Says so right here on page sixty-four."

The all-squeezed-up look left Ian's face. She passed him the book, and he started to thumb through it.

"You think we could really find LaRue's treasure?" he asked.

"Sure," she said, leaning back against the wall. "We can do anything we set our minds to. I heard a man say that on TV the other day. 'Course he was talkin' 'bout winning some election, but I figured all that positive-thinking stuff oughta work for most anybody."

Leastwise, she hoped it did, 'cause she had two particular goals in mind.

The first was to make sure they didn't try to split up her and Ian. Aunt Dale had promised that they wouldn't, but Sean didn't believe her. Grown-ups said a lot of things they didn't mean. That's why you couldn't count on nobody but yourself.

The second was to keep reading her book on pirates and learn all she could about them. One day she and Ian would find LaRue's treasure . . . and a lot of others' too. Then they would use all that gold and silver to buy a place of their own, and maybe a place for Mama, too, after she got better.

"All you gotta do is believe it'll be okay," she told him.

She squeezed her hands into fists.

And she believed.

ONE

Trust no one.

Question everything.

Because things are rarely what they appear at first glance.

Smiling grimly, Dalton Gregory batted at a mosquito buzzing around his face, then ducked under the low-slung limb of a scraggly Florida pine before trudging down the pathway toward the LaRue Expedition campsite.

Even some twenty years later, he still thought it was good advice. *Questioning* everything. In fact, the wisdom of never accepting anything—or anyone—at face value was probably the single best piece of advice Dalton had ever received from his paternal grandfather, Samuel Gregory, a retired high-school history teacher and self-described radical who'd been jailed more than once for questioning the status quo.

A bird began to sing from somewhere deep in the marsh; an unseen animal rustled in the impenetrable thicket of greener-than-green vines and gnarled brown branches nearby, but mostly it was quiet. It was early afternoon in July in Pensacola, and even the wildlife were taking a brief siesta.

Wishing for a breeze, Dalton reached up and loosened the knot in his tie. It did little good. His dress shirt, crisp and cool a short two hours before, now felt soaked with perspiration and clung with equal tenacity both to his skin and to the lining of his brown tweed jacket.

Trying to shrug off his discomfort as well as the unrelenting heat, Dalton skirted a patch of nearly knee-high marsh grass and continued down the overgrown path.

It just didn't make sense, dammit, he thought. Why would his grandfather have agreed to allow some fast-talking treasure hunter a one-year access to his property so she could search for legendary pirate Jackson LaRue's even more legendary hoard of riches?

Worse than that, why would Samuel agree to help *fund* the woman's foolhardy expedition?

Dalton shook his head. *LaRue's treasure? In his grandfather's own backyard?*

"Ridiculous," he muttered.

People had been digging up the coast from Galveston to St. Petersburg for over a hundred years, hoping to find the fortune that wily old pirate supposedly had buried, with virtually no success at all.

For what it was worth—which wasn't a lot in Dalton's opinion—Pensacola was one of the sites most frequently mentioned as a probable hiding place for LaRue's purloined gold and silver. But finding it would require a lot of time and money and even more luck. Samuel's resources were limited, in terms of both money and time, and luck was too capricious a commodity to be counted upon by anyone.

Yet Samuel's new *partner* had confidently promised him that she could have the treasure unearthed within a matter of months.

Yeah, right.

Ten years before, Samuel would have laughed Sean Kilpatrick and her cohorts from Setarip Salvage, Ltd., right out of his house and then called the Pensacola Police Department's bunco squad to discuss lodging a complaint. With a name like Setarip—or pirates, spelled backward—how could *anyone* have taken their outlandish claims seriously?

Two weeks before, however, Samuel had decided to strike a deal with her.

Now Samuel's bank account was some $25,000 lighter, and he was confined to a hospital room with the broken hip he'd gotten from taking a tumble in the marsh while out on this so-called treasure hunt. As for LaRue's lost fortune . . . well, it was still lost.

Big surprise.

Dalton muttered a curse under his breath and swatted at another mosquito.

The worst part of this whole mess was that Dalton couldn't imagine what had gotten into his grandfather. For most of his eighty-one years, Samuel Gregory had practiced what he'd preached. He'd questioned. He'd double-checked the facts. He'd even imagined government conspiracies lurking behind events that most people would have accepted without a second thought.

Samuel had been more than a tad eccentric, but he'd also been the closest thing to a childhood hero Dalton had ever had. Samuel had a way of inspiring passion in those around him.

A passion for the lessons the past could teach.

A passion for protecting the hopes of the future.

What's more, Samuel had been a damn fine teacher. Dalton could only hope that he was doing half as good a job with his own American-history students at the University of Georgia as his grandfather had in his fifty-odd years of teaching.

Rather than reciting a litany of dates and facts for his class to transcribe into notes, Samuel had actually cared about his students. He'd wanted them to excel at life more than he wanted them to excel in high-school history. To achieve that goal, he'd done his level best to teach them the moral behind the historical fact . . . such as the importance of always inspecting any unexpectedly arriving wooden horses for signs of well-hidden Greeks.

Dalton sighed.

Maybe it was simply that old age had finally caught up with Samuel. Maybe he'd begun to lose his grip on his mental faculties, although when Dalton had visited with Samuel at the hospital an hour earlier, he'd seemed anything but senile. Still . . .

Funding a search for the buried pirate treasure of Jackson LaRue?

It was hardly the kind of investment a man who'd once prided himself on his healthy cynicism would become involved with.

The path opened into a small cypress and yellow pine-bordered clearing that had been transformed into a high-tech equipment-laden campsite. The camp was empty, though, except for one person: a tall, leggy redhead working on what appeared to be a large generator next to a tarp-covered bench.

Dalton slowed to a stop and stared at the

woman. Well, at least he knew the answer to the $25,000 question, he thought, his smile returning, grimmer than ever.

It was hormones.

Sean Kilpatrick, CEO of Setarip Salvage, Ltd., and the mastermind behind the LaRue Expedition, was an extraordinarily beautiful woman. Even from a distance of ten or twelve yards, Dalton could tell that. But her beauty wasn't in the heavily made-up mode of some cinematic bombshell.

No, far from it.

Sean's beauty was more fresh and natural, more . . . wholesome, he decided after a moment's reflection.

And more sexy too.

His smile started to lose its grimness. He felt himself begin to relax.

She was a couple of years younger than his thirty-two, although she could pass for a lot younger than that. She had on a lace-trimmed white cotton T-shirt, a pair of cutoff jeans, and work boots, all of which were streaked with equal parts mud and grease from the generator, as were her hands at the moment. Her hair was long and pulled back in a loose French braid that fell down her back. A smudge of black marked the side of one cheek.

Even though she was covered in mud and grease, Dalton couldn't recall a time when he'd seen a more breathtakingly beautiful woman.

Or one who'd captivated his attention so completely without saying a word.

When Samuel had talked about Sean, he'd described her as being an angel.

With the sun reflecting off her hair, making it look like a burnished copper halo, Dalton could well understand his grandfather's reasoning.

Dalton let his gaze slide down her body, deciding that he liked what he saw. But *angel* wasn't the way he would have described her.

He flat out grinned this time.

No, with her slender, athletic build and lightly tanned fair skin, Sean Kilpatrick looked like the proverbial girl next door. He'd even be willing to bet she had a light dusting of freckles across the bridge of her nose, although he was too far away from her to tell for certain. Even without the freckles, she was as all-American as warm apple pie and baseball games in the summertime.

Only he doubted if any man ever thought about apple pies or baseball or anything else when she was around.

Especially when he could be thinking about another favorite American pastime . . . the kind that involved sharing sweet, hot kisses under a moonlit sky.

Rather than do the automatic mental shift

he normally would have, Dalton decided to let the provocative visual image develop a bit further before shutting it off. He imagined himself striding over to her and pulling her hard against his chest . . . imagined her hair tumbling loose from the French braid and spilling around her shoulders.

He imagined himself weaving his fingers through those copper-colored tresses and pulling her face up to kiss her . . . deeply . . . fully.

He imagined the taste of her mouth and the softness of her bare skin.

He could imagine it all . . . and it was all feeling damned good too.

A wave of a different kind of heat crashed over him then, leaving him feeling more than a little disoriented in its wake. He felt his body begin to respond, grow hard. His heart started to race.

"Son-of-a-bitch," he whispered under his breath, amazed at the intensity of his reaction to a woman he didn't know and likely never would.

Forget about Samuel, he told himself. *What the devil is the matter with me?*

Deciding that one Gregory male with a hormonal imbalance was enough for any family, Dalton took a deep breath and refocused his energies on the purpose of his visit. Namely, to recover Samuel's money, if possible, and toss the entire Setarip clan out on their collective ears.

Dalton strode toward her.

"Party's over, sweetheart," he called out.

She froze at the sound of his voice. Her gaze shot toward him, blue eyes wide with surprise. She looked as defenseless as a deer caught in the headlights of an oncoming car.

A stab of guilt for having startled her sliced through him.

Her paralysis proved short-lived, though.

She tossed the grease-covered wrench aside and quickly reached under the tarp. She slid out a twenty-gauge shotgun and pulled herself up straight, then leveled the weapon at him.

The sight stopped him dead in his tracks six feet away from her.

"I'm not your sweetheart," she murmured.

Her voice was Southern femininity at its finest, softly inviting and as soothing as silk. But there was no mistaking its deadly serious tone.

Nor was there any mistaking the ease with which she held the gun.

"And this *party* I'm having is a private one," she added coolly. "Since I don't recall adding your name to the invitation list, maybe you'd better leave."

He folded his arms against his chest and stared her down—or tried to.

He got the impression that no one would likely best Sean Kilpatrick in a battle of wills.

So much for the image of Bambi caught in the headlights, he thought with self-derision. This was one woman who could take care of herself.

"Planning to shoot me?" he asked.

She shrugged. The steely determination in her gaze didn't waver.

Nor did her grip on the gun.

"Guess that depends on you," she said.

She slowly cocked the shotgun and aimed its barrel toward the center of his chest.

Dalton felt his insides grow cold.

"You're trespassing on private property, mister," she said.

A few seconds ticked by.

"I'm not the one trespassing here, Ms. Kilpatrick," he said in a voice just as cool as hers had been. "I'm Dalton Gregory. My grandfather owns this land. I want you and your crew packed up and out of here within the hour. Do I make myself clear?"

She frowned. "You're Sammy's grandson?"

He frowned back at her. "Yes."

She muttered a curse of her own—more imaginative than his had been earlier—and lowered the shotgun.

"Well, why the hell didn't you say so?" she

demanded. "You could give a person heart failure, the way you came barreling in here."

She reached for a rag on the ground next to the generator and wiped the grease from the gun, then slid it back under the edge of the tarp to its resting place under the workbench. She wiped off her hands and tossed the soiled cloth back to the ground. She was acting as though she didn't have a care in the world other than ridding herself of the grease she'd acquired while working on the generator.

She either hadn't heard his order to vacate the property, or she was choosing to ignore him.

He was betting on the latter.

"Tell me, Ms. Kilpatrick, do you always pull a shotgun on visitors to your campsite?"

She laughed.

The sound was as soft as the tinkle of crystal wind chimes, but it was also as free and unrestrained as the wind itself. It was the laugh of a person who joyfully embraced life with both arms wide open.

He decided he liked it.

"Call me Sean," she suggested. "And I'm sorry about the gun, but I thought you were some lunatic claim jumper or worse. We've tried to keep our presence here quiet, but word is bound to leak out. The LaRue treasure has been conservatively estimated to be in the low seven figures. Between the looky-loos and the potential for thieves, a girl's got to protect herself."

His frown deepened. "I thought you had a whole team out here with you."

"Not at this point. Right now it's only me and two others."

She wiped the back of her hand against her perspiration-dampened cheek, noticed the smudge of grease, and walked behind the generator to a large open-sided tent. He followed her.

"I use a small crew when we're in the preliminary stages," she explained. "It's more cost-effective than bringing out the entire team, even if it means I get stuck with doing a lot of the routine maintenance on our generator."

"I see."

Dalton gave the tent a quick once-over. Inside it were several navy-blue folding canvas chairs, a couple of sturdy card tables, and several thousand dollars' worth of intimidating-looking computer equipment and other high-powered gizmos he couldn't even begin to identify. The tent's heavy canvas sides were rolled up and held in place by pieces of thick nylon cord. He assumed that they could be quickly dropped and tied down in case of inclement weather, leaving the expensive equipment inside well protected from the elements.

"My brother Ian had been hung up on a salvage job down in Miami, but he got here last night," she went on. "He and Brian, our geologist, are out in the marsh right now taking some soil samples. I don't expect them back until suppertime."

She plucked a premoistened toilette from an economy pack on the folding metal table and wiped off her face. He'd been right about the freckles, he thought, watching her. Sean definitely had them. Dozens of them. They were like a light sprinkling of copper-colored dust across her cheeks and sunburned nose.

"Soil samples?" he asked, forcing himself to concentrate on what she was saying and not on her freckles . . . or on the incredible blueness of her eyes.

It was damn hard to concentrate, though. His head started to throb from the effort.

She nodded. "Some precious metals give off readings that we can detect by soil analysis, but I'm mostly interested in finding traces of iron or wood from the sea chest. It's Brian's job to verify that any readings we receive are likely to be caused by something *put* into the ground rather than from something occurring there naturally. The site they're testing is one of three I've targeted as a probable location for the treasure. If we get any positive readings, we attempt to verify it with either ground-penetrating radar or a high-powered metal detector before starting to dig."

She dropped the used toilette into a trash can.

"I thought you people were simply going to follow a map," he said.

"Until *X* marked the spot?" She grinned but didn't look up.

"We've got some documents which pinpoint a location," she said, "but finding that location isn't as simple as using a map from the Auto Club. Natural landmarks are usually subject to interpretation. Besides, they can change over the years. Trees get chopped down or struck down by lightning. Rivers can change course. Even rock formations can be altered by natural erosion. That's why we use computers to fill in some of the blanks. Treasure hunting has gone strictly high-tech these days."

She glanced at him and then her expression immediately sobered. "Geez, Dalton, you look like you're roasting in that jacket and tie."

She leaned over and fingered the lapel of his sport coat.

"Tweed?" She laughed again. "It's very professorial and all that, but it's gotta be hotter than hell. Why don't you take it off, roll up your sleeves, and relax before you drop?"

The scent of her perfume nearly did him

in right there on the spot. Its soft floral fragrance felt as familiar as a hug from a lover. It wrapped around him, making his knees feel weak and his head throb all the more. His heart started to pound in earnest now.

Then her fingertips casually brushed against his shirt. The heat of her touch seared through the damp fabric and sizzled his skin, bringing all those naughty fantasies he'd been enjoying about her earlier crashing back with a vengeance.

He felt himself flush straight down to his toes.

Her gaze locked with his.

"Are you okay?" she asked, her expression filled with concern.

"I . . . I'm fine," he lied.

Although the longer he stood so close to her, inhaling her perfume, feeling her touch— impersonal though it was—the less chance he figured he had of being able to lie successfully.

She stared at him a little longer, then nodded toward the canvas chair next to him.

"Well, I'd feel better if you took a seat. You don't look so good to me."

She turned away and opened the door to a battered mini-refrigerator. She took out a couple of plastic bottles, one filled with plain water and the other a popular store brand of a beverage used by athletes to restore an electrolyte imbalance. She tossed him the latter.

"You're probably dehydrated," she added. "You should drink something before you pass out. Tramping through a swamp in tweed in ninety-plus temperatures is a good way to get heatstroke, you know."

She sank down in a chair and unscrewed the cap on her own water.

He didn't say anything. He just stared, not sure what he should make of her . . . or of himself for that matter. He'd already decided that she probably wasn't a con artist out to fleece Samuel out of his life savings, but that still didn't change the fact that Setarip was too risky a venture for Samuel to become involved with.

However, what bothered Dalton most about her was his own response. He'd never felt such an immediate attraction to a woman as he did to Sean . . . and he wasn't all that sure that he liked feeling that way.

The throbbing in his head grew stronger.

He lifted the cool bottle and rolled it across his forehead, luxuriating in the dozens of icy shivers that followed. Then he unscrewed its cap, raised the bottle, and took a long swallow.

He followed it with another and started to feel better. Heat, humidity, and a tweed jacket were a lethal combination, he reminded himself as the headache slowly began to subside. Could be Sean was right about the heatstroke.

After all, what he'd been feeling—the dizziness, the heart palpitations, the slight disorientation whenever she was a tad too close to him—were all classic symptoms.

Then she shifted her position in the chair, causing her T-shirt to stretch tautly across her full, rounded breasts.

He felt his body tighten again . . . and knew that heatstroke was the least of his problems.

"You, ah, did hear what I said a couple of minutes ago, didn't you?" he asked, giving the bottle another roll across his forehead.

She gave him a blank look.

"About what?" she asked.

"I said I want you packed and off the property within an hour."

She grinned. "Oh, that." She took a swig of water. "Yeah, I heard."

"And?"

She shrugged. "I assumed you must be joking . . . or just delusional from the heat. I've got a signed contract with your grandfather. We're partners."

"Contracts can be broken."

"Not without a good reason, they can't."

He regarded her for a moment.

"I can think of several good reasons for doing it," he said.

"I'd settle for just one."

"Okay," he said, taking a deep breath.

"How about the impaired thought process on the part of one of the signatories? A beautiful woman . . . a lonely old man . . . a judge might think it sort of makes for an unfair balance of power."

Now it was her turn to regard him.

Seconds ticked by.

"Yeah," she said finally. "It's definitely heatstroke." She paused another millisecond or two. " 'Cause if I thought you were serious about what you'd just accused me of doing . . . well, I'd be coldcocking you so fast, you wouldn't have a chance to see what hit you."

She set her water bottle onto the ground next to her feet.

"Now, sit down, Dalton," she drawled, sounding unbearably smug and self-assured. "Take off your damn jacket and drink up."

She flashed him a grin. "You really need to cool off before you make an even bigger ass of yourself."

TWO

Sean Kilpatrick slowly leaned back in her canvas chair and crossed her legs, keeping her gaze locked on Dalton's face.

Although his words had stung, she couldn't say she really blamed him for being suspicious of her or the LaRue Expedition. Suspicion was a natural response to a world filled with an ever-increasing number of hustlers and scam artists who targeted the elderly.

The fact that she considered Sammy to be the least likely person she knew ever to fall for a con of any kind was actually beside the point.

After all, Dalton didn't know her from Adam, or rather Eve. What little Dalton did know about her and her partnership with Sammy had probably made him extremely nervous. Why, if she'd been in his position, she knew she would have been apprehensive and then some. She imagined he wouldn't waste much time in having both her and Setarip checked out.

Which was fine by her.

She welcomed the scrutiny.

There were two things Sean prided herself on doing well. First was marine salvage. Thanks to the long hours of hard work she and her brother had spent as apprentices learning the business from the ground floor up, their company, Setarip Salvage, Ltd., enjoyed an unblemished reputation within its service area of the Gulf Coast and eastern seaboard. They got the job done as fast and economically as possible without compromising safety.

The second—and probably far more reassuring item from Dalton's likely perspective—was her experience as a professional treasure hunter. She specialized in recovering the lost booty of seventeenth- and eighteenth-century pirates.

She was damned good at it, too, if she did say so herself.

Rather than investing in college, Sean had spent countless hours studying pirates on her own. She had analyzed every scrap of information she could get her hands on, from outlandish bits of folklore to journal entries filled with probable half-truths, all in an attempt to uncover subtle clues to the location of their buried—or sunken—treasure.

Since Setarip's occasional foray into the quest for that treasure had produced more hits than it had misses in the last seven years, she figured she must be doing something right.

She also figured that her research into pirates had given her something of an edge when it came to spotting the modern-day variety.

She let her gaze slowly slide down Dalton's six-foot frame, moving from the perspiration-dampened waves of his short dark brown hair, down the chiseled bone structure of his much-too-handsome face, to his broad shoulders, flat stomach, and slim hips.

Oh, there was no doubt about it, she decided with another grin.

Dalton Gregory—the same Dalton Gregory that Sammy had once described to her as being a much-too-sensible-for-his-own-good professor of American history—was the living, breathing embodiment of every pirate legend she'd ever read about.

Especially when he glared at her the way he was doing right now. There was even a glint in his gray eyes that could only be described as murderous.

It was the kind of scowl she'd always imagined Blackbeard had displayed right before he'd boarded a soon-to-be-captured ship.

Truth be told, though, she'd have probably stood a better chance of survival with Blackbeard.

Dalton looked as though he wanted to make her walk the plank . . . and the little fact that they weren't onboard a ship at the present time didn't seem to be bothering him in the least.

She wouldn't have been at all surprised if he tried to make do by tying a chunk of limestone around her neck, then pushing her off an ol' cypress stump into the largest sinkhole he could find.

Dalton muttered an expletive packing enough venom, it could have peeled the paint right off the walls of her condominium back in Key Biscayne.

Then he did as she'd strongly urged him to two times. He stripped off his jacket and tossed it across a nearby chair.

"You must think this is some kind of a joke," he said, clipping his words with razor-sharp precision. "But I've got some serious concerns about both you and this expedition of yours, Sean."

His voice was deep and rich and utterly masculine, and she didn't doubt him for a second when he said he was concerned about his grandfather's welfare.

She also didn't doubt that Dalton would

likely fight her to the death if he thought she had somehow wronged Sammy in the deal.

But pirates had a way of commanding that kind of respect, she reminded herself . . . and Dalton's voice had those same piratelike qualities.

With very little effort at all, she could imagine it bellowing across the bow of a ship in the heat of battle, sending fear shooting straight into the hearts of hapless sailors on the vessel under fire.

She could also imagine that same voice filling the small confines of the captain's quarters late at night with the softly whispered promises of all kinds of forbidden sensual pleasures. . . .

Just as she could imagine the shivers of sheer anticipatory delight that would tumble down the spine of the woman lucky enough to have him whispering those things to her.

Heat crept into Sean's cheeks, but she immediately shut off the devilishly seductive images. Fantasizing about pirates was one thing. Fantasizing about romantic gobbledygook was quite another.

She frowned. She must have been out in the sun a tad too long today herself, she thought, trying to rationalize her unexpected flight of erotic fancy.

She didn't believe in any of that pulse-begins-to-quicken-whenever-*he*-walks-into-the-room nonsense, and yet here she was going all goo-goo-eyed over Dalton like some love-struck teenager.

She told herself to knock it off.

She uncrossed her legs, stiffened her spine, and sat up a bit straighter.

"I'm sorry," she told him. "I didn't mean to make light of your concerns about Sammy. I imagine it must have been very frightening for you to receive the call about his accident."

Dalton met her gaze. "Not nearly as frightening as learning about its cause, believe me."

She decided to let the barb slide.

"But you're right," he said. "Getting the call from the hospital . . ."

He took a deep breath. "It scared the crap out of me," he finished, giving a humorless chuckle.

"I guess I'd always thought of Samuel as being indestructible," he went on. "Finding out he'd broken his hip was probably the first time I'd realized just how old and frail he'd really become. It . . . it's been a while since I've been down for a visit. Classes, committee meetings, they've been consuming a lot of my time lately."

"So, naturally, when the call came from the hospital, you started to feel guilty for not having been to visit him earlier?"

"Something like that," he murmured. "He

and my father had a falling-out years ago over politics. They haven't spoken since. There aren't any other grandchildren, so there really is no one else to care about him. I feel like I let him down."

She felt a slight tug on her heart but didn't say anything.

Dalton loosened his tie, slid it off, and tossed it onto the chair on top of his jacket.

"Tell me something, Sean," he said, his voice coldly serious. "Why did you agree to let him tag along on your little adventure? The man is eighty-one years old, for Pete's sake."

She reached down and snagged her water bottle.

"Yeah, and he's in better physical shape than most men thirty years younger," she countered, unscrewing the cap to the bottle.

"And just how would you suggest that I might have prevented him from *tagging along*, as you put it?" she asked. "He'd invested in the expedition. We're going to be digging on his land. He had a right to be here—both legally and morally. We even had a clause in our contract that guaranteed him access."

She took a sip of water. Besides, she thought, she liked having him around. Sammy had a boundless energy that seemed to miraculously recharge the batteries of those around him.

Dalton tugged his shirt out from the waistband of his trousers and started to unbutton it.

Sean watched him undress, feeling almost hypnotized. It was as though her gaze were being pulled to his chest like some tiny paper clip drawn to a magnet the size of Mt. Rushmore.

And it was a nice chest, too, she decided as each button came undone. It was firm, tanned, and tightly muscled, with a thatch of dark brown hair that tapered down to his belly button.

She concentrated on his belly for a moment. He had flat, well-defined abs. Not the kind of rippled hardness that only seemed to occur in male models, but the kind that was a natural part of a well-toned physique.

She watched his fingers fumble with the buttons and wondered for an insane moment or two if she should offer to help him.

Although touching him was probably not the wisest move she could ever make.

Especially since she seemed to have this almost all-consuming need to find out whether his chest hair would be as soft to the touch as it looked. . . .

Or if his tightly muscled arms would feel as good wrapped tightly around her body as she was imagining they would feel.

Her mouth went dry. Her heart started to

pound. Then she blushed until she was certain her face was the same color as her hair.

Oh, get a grip, she told herself in mounting exasperation.

She was acting as though she'd never seen a man's bare chest before, when she had. Hundreds of times. Most of the guys she worked with walked around in either just their swim trunks or a pair of cutoffs. And a lot of them had great bodies.

But it was the thought of Dalton's body that was firing her imagination into an erotic meltdown.

She found it damned annoying that he seemed to be oblivious of the effect his seminudity was having upon her.

"I guess I'm just not making myself clear here," he said.

He settled himself into his chair and took another drink. The sides to his shirt fluttered closed, restricting her view of his chest.

Sean took a deep breath, held it for a long moment, then slowly exhaled. She forced herself to concentrate on what he was saying.

"No, I guess you're not," she told him. "What, exactly, is the problem here?"

"My grandfather lives on a fixed income," he said. "He can't afford to invest in the La-Rue Expedition because he can't afford to lose the money. I don't know what he was thinking when he agreed to do it, but he was obviously not thinking clearly."

"I . . . see."

"That's why I'd like for you to do the honorable thing. Refund his money and call off this idiotic search for pirate treasure."

She took a slow swallow of water, wondering how she was going to answer him.

In the end, she decided to go with the truth.

"Sorry, Dalton, I couldn't do that even if I wanted to," she said. "The money is already spent. Nonrefundable equipment rentals. Permits. That kind of thing. Besides, calling off the search at this point would be . . . well, it would be insane, considering all the time and money we've all invested."

"And this wild-goose chase of yours is supposed to be *sane*, I take it?"

"Yes," she said. "In fact, it's extremely sane and rational and well thought out."

She shook her head. "You act as though you think this is some scheme I came up with two weeks ago or something. It's not. I've been researching the details of this expedition for years."

It had been more like two thirds of her lifetime, but she saw no reason to mention that part.

"I've made it my business to get to know Jackson LaRue," she went on. "I know what he liked to drink when he was feeling sad and I know the name of the tailor who made his clothes. I also know that he left behind a considerable fortune in gold, silver, and jewels which he'd divided into three wooden chests and buried to prevent their capture by the British in late June of 1813. LaRue was killed a month later in a dramatic sea battle off the coast of Florida. It was thought the location of those three chests died with him. Thanks to his mistress's journal, however, I've got a pretty damn good idea where at least one of them is."

Dalton leaned forward, his gray eyes sparking with sudden interest.

"Wait a minute," he said. "Is this the map that Samuel was referring to? You have a copy of Elizabeth Martene's journal?"

"Yes."

Sean was impressed that he even knew who Elizabeth was, since the name hadn't registered at all with Sammy. Elizabeth Martene, the seventeen-year-old daughter of a Pensacola landowner, had been but a small chapter in the life of Jackson LaRue and an even smaller footnote in the annals of history.

"I acquired the journal last year at an auction in New Orleans," she said. "Most of it concerns her day-to-day life, boring stuff actually, but several passages concern LaRue.

Elizabeth's literary style was a bit florid when she described their assignations."

She rolled her eyes at the memory.

"What interested me was her recounting of the burial of one of the chests," she explained. "She was apparently an eyewitness. She said she'd helped him 'plant the golden seed for their future' in marshlands outside of Pensacola near the spot where they'd first made love.

"Now, rumor has it that their first sexual encounter took place in a trapper's hut out near some limestone caverns," she went on. "Caves are rare in Pensacola. They are more plentiful the closer you get to Tallahassee. Since there weren't many caverns in this area, it wasn't too hard to narrow the search down to about three acres of wetlands around Pensacola."

"Which, coincidentally, all happen to be in my grandfather's backyard," Dalton said.

"Bingo."

He took another drink but didn't say anything.

She rescrewed the cap and set the water bottle back on the ground.

"Dalton, I know searching for LaRue's treasure is a risk," she said quietly. "Setarip has a large portion of its own funds invested in this. *I* have a large portion of *my* funds invested in this. And just for the record, Sammy knew what he was getting into. I never asked that he invest. I only wanted his permission to conduct the recovery. Investing was his idea."

She shrugged. "He said he was ready and willing to take the chance. He said that he wanted to have one last adventure before he got too old to enjoy them. I took him at his word. I believe he meant it. I still do. So I agreed to let him invest. For what it's worth," she added, "my gut feeling is that the treasure is here. Given enough time, I know that we can find that chest."

"I thought you told Samuel that this whole operation would take only a couple of months."

"No, I told him that the first stage should take only a couple of months," she corrected. "That will include the areas I've targeted as having the strongest fit with the description in Elizabeth's journal. If my calculations are correct, we'll find the chest. But if they're wrong . . . well, then it could probably take us years to find the actual spot."

"Assuming, of course, that Elizabeth's journal is accurate," he said.

"Exactly. But I've no reason at this point to think otherwise."

She smoothed back a flyaway tendril of her hair.

"Look, I don't know what else I can say. I've got the credentials to do the job. Setarip has done these kind of recoveries before, though not for a prize of this magnitude. You can check us out with the state."

"I plan to," he said matter-of-factly. "In the meantime, it looks as though my only viable option for protecting Samuel's investment is to allow the LaRue Expedition to continue."

She drew a sigh of relief. Even though there wasn't much Dalton could have done to stop her and Setarip—especially since she doubted that Sammy was even aware of what his grandson was up to—Dalton did have the power to make her life miserable.

Better make that *beyond* miserable, she decided after thinking about it for a second.

"Thanks," she said.

"Oh, don't thank me yet," he told her. "I still think this is a ridiculous idea, but it's apparently an idea we're stuck with for the time being."

There was something about the way he said *for the time being* that suddenly made her extremely nervous.

"And as long as we're stuck with it," he went on, "I suppose we might as well set out some ground rules for the next couple of months. We can start by discussing the sleeping arrangements."

"Sleeping arrangements?"

"You said that Samuel had both the legal

and moral right to participate in the expedition," he reminded her. "His days of tramping through marshes are over, at least for a couple of months until his hip heals. He's going to need someone to fill in for him, watch over his investment. That kind of thing."

He finished off his drink and set the empty bottle on the ground next to him.

"I won't have any classes until the fall, and I was planning to take a vacation anyway. There's no reason at all why I can't spend my summer here in Pensacola."

Then he gave her a smile that was filled with the kind of sly, sexy charm that pirates were famous for the world over.

"So," he murmured. "About those sleeping arrangements. Should I provide my own tent and sleeping bag, or do you have an extra one that I can use?"

"And you agreed?"

Ian's voice threatened to break the sound barrier when she filled him in a couple of hours later about their new partner's scheduled arrival bright and early the next morning.

His screech of outrage was so loud, a pair of blackbirds perched on the limb of a cypress tree squawked in indignant protest before taking off in flight.

Sean wished she could do the same. The

last thing she felt she needed right then was an argument with her baby brother, who, although the same height as she was, outweighed her by a good fifty pounds.

She'd already fought in one battle today and had the scars to prove it.

Ian skimmed his hand across the top of his close-cropped red hair. "I don't know what's gotten into you lately," he said, shaking his head. "You used to refuse all requests from investors to sit in on the recovery missions. Then you agreed to let Sammy join us. Now you've agreed to let his grandson join in. I don't get it."

"Don't start with me, Mudbug," she warned, calling him by his childhood nickname. "I had no other choice but to agree to Dalton's request. The contract states that Sammy can be an active participant in the expedition. If he wants to have Dalton fill in for him in his absence, it's well within his rights to do so."

Besides, she more than appreciated Dalton's concern about Sammy. Family was important. She understood that better than anyone. Involving himself in the expedition was the only thing Dalton felt he could do to prove he cared, and she respected his decision.

But that still didn't mean that she had to like it, and she didn't.

In fact, the thought of spending nearly every waking moment for the next couple of months with Dalton Gregory was beginning to fill her with dread.

The memory of a firm, well-muscled chest and a voice as beguiling as the devil's own had been haunting her ever since he'd left.

Ian shook his head again. "But—"

She scowled. "No buts," she said, cutting him off. "Dalton Gregory will be here tomorrow morning."

She turned and stalked off toward her tent.

"Deal with it," she shouted at her brother over her shoulder.

Hell, if she had to, she figured everybody else might as well.

THREE

When Dalton arrived at the campsite shortly after eight the next morning, he found Sean sitting at one of the folding card tables in the open-sided tent, poring over a stack of handwritten notes as though they contained the secret to eternal life itself.

He stopped inside the tent and waited for her to notice him . . . although from the way she was so engrossed in her work, he doubted if she would be able to notice anything short of a hurricane with hundred-mile-an-hour winds.

He smiled.

She had her long hair pulled back into another loose French braid, and she was wearing a pale blue scoop-necked T-shirt tucked into a pair of cutoff jeans. She had on the same pair of work boots from the day before, minus most of the mud and grease.

He let his gaze slide over her, deciding to indulge in a bit of good, old-fashioned male appreciation. With her copper-colored hair and fair skin, she looked good in blue. Damned good.

Or rather, he quickly amended, she looked damned good in that T-shirt. His smile turned into an almost lecherous grin.

The T-shirt molded itself to her slender body . . . accentuating her slim waist . . . hugging the soft curves of her breasts.

His gaze lingered on her breasts for a moment. He found himself watching the gentle rise and fall of her chest as she breathed. Before very long, he found himself starting to wonder how she would look unclothed . . . with her shirt and bra lying discarded on the ground beside her.

He started to wonder if her unbound breasts would mold themselves against his palms the way they were molding themselves to her T-shirt now.

Would she softly moan his name in that lilting Southern drawl of hers if he were to begin to stroke her body with his hands . . . then taste her with his mouth . . . until he'd explored every part of her?

His body began to tighten, grow hard. His heart started to pound.

That wave of familiar heat swamped him again, until the simple act of breathing seemed to take every ounce of his energy.

This time he knew what he was feeling wasn't caused by a mild case of heatstroke, since the temperature outside had barely reached the mid-seventies.

No, this was all due to Sean Kilpatrick herself.

He wanted her.

Big time.

Somehow he thought that the realization of that desire should have bothered him a helluva lot more than it was.

"Good morning," came a cheerful-sounding male voice from the rear of the tent.

It snapped Dalton out of his erotic reverie like a bucket of ice water thrown on a sleepwalker.

He glanced toward the back of the tent, surprised to discover that there was anyone else there, although he supposed he really shouldn't have been. With Sean around, he found concentrating on much of anything else to be nearly impossible.

The greeting had come from a slender, balding brown-haired man in his early forties. He sat in front of one of the makeshift workstations behind Sean, inputting a stack of what appeared to be analytic data into one of their high-tech computers.

Dalton nodded a greeting. "Morning."

He dropped his duffel bag to the ground. It landed with a thud on the grass next to his feet.

Sean shuffled her notes into a neat pile, then pushed herself away from the desk and stood. She slowly walked toward him.

"Hi," she said.

The smile she gave him was warm, yet restrained. Almost impersonal.

Even so, it threatened to trigger a whole new batch of those erotic daydreams he'd been bombarded with since meeting her the day before.

"Sorry," she went on. "I was caught up in some paperwork. I, ah, didn't see you come in."

"That's . . . okay," he murmured, wondering if his voice sounded as husky to her ears as it did to his own.

"I just got here," he added.

If she thought he sounded funny, she didn't show it. Instead, she nodded toward the man working at the computer terminal.

"Dalton, meet Brian Redfield, Setarip's chief geologist. Brian, Dalton Gregory. He's Sammy's grandson."

Brian raised his coffee mug, which was emblazoned with the logo of the Miami Dolphins, in a brief salute.

"Welcome aboard," he said. "Next time

you talk to Sammy, please tell him we miss him, and I hope he feels like his old self real soon."

Dalton smiled. "Thanks. I will."

Brian nodded, then returned his attention to the computer.

Dalton glanced back at Sean.

Their gazes locked, held.

Seconds passed.

A warm breeze floated through the open-sided tent, sending a few long tendrils of her hair flying onto her face . . . and causing the soft scent of her perfume to waft around him.

He felt his abdominal muscles begin to tighten.

Suddenly the need to reach out and pull her into his arms for a kiss nearly overpowered his senses.

She seemed to know it, too, as an awareness of him as a man started to grow in her eyes. There was more than mere comprehension of his need for her, though. There was also a hunger as strong as his own.

She wanted him.

He was as certain of this fact as he'd been of anything in his entire life.

She blushed and quickly glanced away. "Umm, let me show you to your tent."

Then she turned and headed out to the main encampment without another word.

Taking a deep breath—damn, if he didn't

get a grip on himself soon, he'd probably need a cold shower before lunch—he picked up his duffel bag and followed her.

They walked the short distance to the row of tents, each set up approximately five feet from the other. His was the one farthest to the right. He wasn't sure which one belonged to Brian or Ian, but there was little doubt that the one next to Dalton's was Sean's. The clothes she'd worn the day before were lying in a laundry hamper right outside the flap of her tent.

"The communal showers are next to that stand of cypress trees," she said, pointing out the location to him. "We have to conserve hot water, so there's a three-minute limit on showers. Bathroom facilities are next door."

He nodded.

"Supplies are kept in a metal cabinet next to the showers," she went on, as though reciting from a mental list she used when indoctrinating new additions to her expeditions.

"Everyone cleans up after themselves," she said. "No wet towels on the floor of the stall, in other words. Laundry's done once a week. Everyone takes a turn. Same with meals. Any questions?"

"Nope," he said.

He dropped the duffel bag onto the ground and pushed it inside the tent with the tip of his sneaker. Then he glanced back at her.

Their gazes locked.

"So . . ." He let his voice trail off. He started to smile.

She blushed again. "So . . ."

More seconds passed.

He knew he should say something to her. Anything. Perhaps ask her what she thought he could do to help with the search for La-Rue's treasure chest. After all, ensuring the success of the expedition was the reason Dalton was there.

Wasn't it?

He cleared his throat. "So . . . is Brian doing the soil analysis from the potential sites?"

It was a pointless question, he knew, since it was blatantly obvious that was what Brian had been doing. But it was the first thing that had popped into Dalton's mind that had seemed halfway intelligible, so he'd decided to go with it.

She quickly nodded as though relieved by the break in the tension between them.

"Right," she told him, making the word sound as though it suddenly had two syllables instead of one.

"We won't have any conclusive reports for a while, though," she added. "Ian's out picking up a batch of soil samples from the third location, which Brian will start analyzing to-morrow."

"I see."

He sought out her gaze again. "What about you? Planning to tackle that mountain of paperwork I pulled you away from?" he teased.

She smiled. "Not right now. I was cooped up in the camp all yesterday. I'm planning to head out to the cavern and double-check some coordinates as soon as I get you settled in."

He gave her a grin this time, then tapped his duffel bag with the toe of his sneaker.

"Consider me settled," he said. "I'm good to go whenever you are, sweetheart."

"You're good to . . . ?"

She stared at him for a moment, then took a slow, deep breath as though she were count-ing to ten.

"That's . . . great," she said, although the tone in her voice told him that she thought his suggestion of joining her was any-thing but.

"Let's go."

Sean told herself that she should have shot Dalton while she'd had the chance and gotten the whole thing over and done with.

After having trekked with him through a partial pine forest and a whole lot of wetlands for the past fifteen minutes, she thought it was downright amazing that she still had a grip, shaky though it was, on what remained of her sanity.

What made it so amazing was that the man seemed determined to make her certifiably insane.

At times, he'd walked so close to her in a path barely suitable for one that his body heat had sent her own blood pressure rising and the spicy scent of his aftershave had threatened to steal her very breath.

Then, when his shoulder accidentally brushed against hers as they'd rounded a bend in the marsh-grass-lined path, the brief contact of his body against hers had sent enough electrically charged sparks crackling down her spine, she imagined it could have set fire to an entire pine forest.

The worst part was she could have sworn that he was doing it on purpose. It was as though he knew precisely the kind of effect he was having upon her and was taking wicked delight in tormenting her.

She scowled and kicked at a pinecone.

This wasn't the way she'd envisioned things would be once he'd joined the expedition, dammit.

He wasn't supposed to have gotten better looking in a single day, nor was his desirability index supposed to have tripled with a change in wardrobe. She shot him a glance out of the corner of her eye.

His black short-sleeved T-shirt seemed to fit his rock-hard chest like a second skin, and the khaki shorts he wore were the perfect accompaniment to his leanly muscular legs.

Her breath caught in her throat. Her abdominal muscles began to constrict.

This . . . oh, this was ridiculous, she told herself, forcing her attention back to the path.

She did so just in time too.

She'd gotten to the part in the trail where a long-since-uprooted tree blocked their passage.

Without missing a beat, she grabbed one of the tree's rotting limbs and started to pull herself up and over the obstacle. She'd just about made it when her foot began to slip on the moss-covered trunk.

Sean let out a curse and teetered, her arms flailing wildly. The strap of her canvas carryall slipped off her shoulder. The bag fell to one side of the tree trunk while she toppled back toward the other.

"Don't worry," Dalton reassured her.

She felt his arms slide around her waist moments before she slumped against his tightly muscled chest. Then he held her fast in an embrace so close, so intimate, it swamped her senses, sending her pulse racing madly and her heart pounding so fast, she thought that it might jump straight out of her chest.

His hips were pressed against her buttocks. His palms were splayed out on either side of her abdomen. The warmth of their combined pressure burned through the fabric of her shorts to sear her skin, as though it were mere rice paper and he an open flame.

Her throat constricted. Liquid heat began to pool in her lower abdomen.

Oh, dear God, what is happening to me?

She struggled to get out of his grasp.

"It's okay," he said.

His voice was as darkly seductive as sin, his breath a caress against her ear.

"I've got you, sweetheart."

A shudder racked her body at his words. It was exactly what she was afraid of most—that Dalton had indeed *got* her.

She made a grab for the limb of the tree and tried to pull herself back onto the trunk.

Dalton held her tight for a moment, as though he didn't want to release her, then he slid his hands around her waist and gave her a push. She regained her footing and his hands fell away.

"Thanks," she muttered, then jumped to the ground on the other side of the tree as though the devil himself were after her.

❖━━━━━❖

By the time they reached the pine-and-shrub-shrouded entrance to the cavern some five minutes later, Sean was feeling more in control of her emotions. Verifying the accuracy of the coordinates for the dig was too important a task to screw up because of overactive hormones.

She dropped the carryall as close to the actual center of the small clearing as she could estimate it and knelt down. She unzipped the bag and removed the surveying equipment, a leather case containing a pair of binoculars, a sheaf of notes she'd transcribed from Elizabeth's journal, and a pencil.

She stood and started to set up the tripod.

Dalton propped himself against the pine tree and folded his arms against his chest.

"The trapper's hut was dead east about a hundred yards," he offered.

She glanced at him and smiled. "I'm impressed. It looks like you've done your homework."

She screwed in the theodolite to the tripod, then adjusted the position of its small telescope and verified that she'd start with a level reading.

He shrugged. "You're not the only one who ever researched Jackson LaRue," he told her. "When I was a kid, I was even convinced he'd buried his treasure somewhere in Samuel's cave. I spent a whole two weeks one summer vacation searching for it."

Her smile deepened. "So you got bitten by the same bug that bit me?"

"I guess. Though obviously its bite didn't affect me as much. . . . I grew out of it."

She didn't say anything. Instead, she marked her first coordinate, then reached for the leather case containing the binoculars and unsnapped the lid. She removed the binoculars and slowly surveyed the scraggly pine-covered terrain even though she probably knew it by heart.

"So tell me about yourself," he suggested quietly. "Tell me why you do marine salvage. Tell me why you became a professional treasure hunter."

She kept the binoculars trained on the horizon.

"Not a lot to tell, really," she told him. "Marine salvage provides a steady paycheck between the treasure hunts. As for why I like to hunt for treasure . . . well, it's all I've ever thought about doing, ever since I was a kid."

"You're lucky. Most kids' dreams end when they become adults. They have to take sensible jobs, be responsible."

She lowered the binoculars and glanced at him, wondering if he was talking about himself. Sammy had spoken of Dalton often in the two weeks he'd been with the expedition. He had told her how proud he'd been of his grandson's academic accomplishments but that he wished he didn't take life quite so seriously.

"I think that's sad," she said. "Dreams are so very important. They're what keep us believing in the future when we're young, what keep us hanging on for another day when we're old. I know that holding on to my dreams when I was a kid helped get me through some rough spots."

"How so?"

She dropped her gaze. "When I was ten, my dad died." She took a deep breath. "He'd been depressed for a long time. He'd lost his job, had a problem with alcohol. My mom didn't take his suicide all that well."

"I'm sorry, Sean," he said quietly. "That must have been awful for you."

She shrugged. "We were strong kids. We were used to taking care of ourselves, but yeah, it was all pretty awful. It's not the kind of thing a kid should ever have to deal with."

She ran her fingertips along the binoculars' nylon cord, smoothing out a crimp. "We were living in Louisiana at the time," she went on. "We really didn't have a lot of close family, just great-aunts, uncles, and cousins, and all of them were in Florida. Every time we thought we'd finally found a permanent home, we'd have to pack up and move to the next name on the list. We were shuffled from one relative to the next like some kind of white elephant no one wanted to keep. Still, it could have been worse . . . we were never split up."

Even though several relatives had tried to do it more than once, Sean had firmly stood her ground each time until they'd had to back down. She'd made a promise to herself and to her brother that she'd keep them together, no matter what.

Knowing that she had kept that promise was a source of pride for her.

"But living in Florida had a lot of advantages for treasure-hunters-in-training," she added. Her mood began to lighten. She started to smile. "You see, somewhere along the line we'd figured out that more pirate gold is underwater than underground. Since most of the relatives lived near the water, we were able to get in a lot of diving experience. We were out there nearly every day, looking for sunken ships."

He gave her a warm smile. She felt herself begin to relax even more.

"And I take it that these daily dives of yours eventually paid off?" he asked.

"Oh, yeah," she said, unable to resist a grin. "I made my first big find when I was eighteen. I'd found a possible lead on the location of an old Spanish galleon my senior year of high school. The *Mariana* had been returning from South America with a payload in silver when she'd run into a hurricane and sank, back in the early 1700s. The summer after graduation, my brother and I took a bus down to the Keys to investigate my theories. We found the ship on the fourth dive."

She gave herself a mental hug as the memory of the excitement and the thrill of that first big find washed over her.

"We pulled up most of the silver ourselves," she went on. "It took us weeks. It was all labor-intensive, and we were the labor force. We couldn't afford any of the expensive salvage equipment and we were too afraid to tell anyone about the find for fear they'd take it over, so we had to do it all ourselves. Fortunately, the *Mariana* had come to rest in shallow water."

"I think I remember hearing about it in the news," he murmured.

He pushed himself away from the tree and walked toward her.

"Weren't there several so-called professionals out searching for the *Mariana*?" he asked. "I seem to recall a lot of them had gotten angry that a couple of kids had succeeded where they couldn't."

She laughed. "Yeah, but they'd been searching in all the wrong places. They'd misread the records in the Spanish archives. Still,

I was lucky. I had a lot to learn about the business."

She lifted the nylon strap over her head and set the binoculars on the ground next to the notes.

"That's why I didn't open Setarip right away," she told him. "We had the money to do it, but I didn't feel we had enough training or practical experience. So I took a job with another marine salvage operation in the Keys and learned the ropes. My brother did the same once he graduated from high school. I apprenticed for five years before going out on my own. Setarip's been in business for seven years now. I think we've done fairly well for ourselves," she added modestly.

"Fairly well?"

He started to laugh. The sound was hearty and rich. It was a man's laugh, she decided, feeling every nuance of its masculinity deep inside her feminine core.

A pirate's laugh.

"From what I've heard, you've done more than just well, Sean," he said, taking her hand.

He gave it a warm, gentle squeeze. It was a casual gesture, but soon its comforting warmth had turned into something much hotter.

"I, ah, gather that you placed those phone calls you were talking about," she said, trying her damnedest to keep her voice even and steady. But something told her she was failing miserably in the attempt.

She eased her hand out of his grasp.

"That I did," he said.

"And?"

"I liked what I discovered," he said, giving her another one of his warm, comforting smiles. "You have a reputation for not taking foolish risks."

"You can't afford to in this business," she murmured. Just like in real life, she thought—especially with men like Dalton Gregory.

"Hmm. I guess ol' Samuel hasn't lost his mind as completely as I'd thought," Dalton teased, reaching for her hand again.

He started to slide his thumb along her palm in a slow, lazy circle. The touch was gentle, barely perceptible, but it packed enough of a fire-laced wallop to set her entire body aflame.

She could feel the burn straight through to the marrow of her bones.

"Oh?" she murmured.

Her heart started to beat at a rapid-fire pace.

"You mean you don't think I'm some con artist out to steal your grandfather's money anymore?"

"Of course not. I stopped thinking that ten minutes into our first conversation."

He grinned and leaned closer until his face

was less than a breath away from hers. He raised his free hand and cupped her chin in its palm.

"Now I think the only thing you're probably capable of stealing is a man's heart," he said. "Along with a bit of his sanity too."

She felt herself start to flush.

"Don't be ridiculous," she said.

"Is it so ridiculous?" he asked, his voice dropping lower, huskier. The sound seemed to caress her and torture her at the same time.

"You see . . ." He took a ragged breath. "I'm not all that sure myself."

He slowly brushed his lips against her cheek. She shuddered.

"Do you have any idea what you do to me, Sean?" he murmured huskily. "Do you know how crazy you've been driving me these past twenty-four hours? Do you know how much I want to touch you? How much I want to kiss you?"

His voice was rough, streaked with a need and a hunger that she felt all too acutely herself.

Then he stroked her cheek with his fingertips, sending hundreds of white-hot shivers shooting down her spine that felt as though they would likely melt her soul with their intensity.

"I . . . oh, I think I've got a good idea," she told him.

After all, she'd been feeling all of those same things about him.

He brushed his lips against her cheek again.

"But I also think it'd be even crazier if we allowed ourselves to act upon any of those impulses," she added huskily.

His response was to tighten his grip on her hand and pull her closer until she was pressed against his body, breasts to chest, belly to belly. The heat swirled around her until it was all she knew.

"Probably," he murmured.

His gray eyes had darkened to the color of midnight. He slowly released her hand and reached up to clasp her chin in both palms.

"Thing is, sweetheart," he said, "I guess I just don't care anymore . . . 'cause all I can think about is how much I want to kiss you right now."

Then he tilted her chin up and captured her mouth in a kiss unlike any other she'd known before.

She surrendered to him, letting herself get lost in the power and the beauty of the kiss for a moment. She luxuriated in the delicious sensations created by his warm, soft lips, his demanding tongue, and his hard body pressed intimately to hers. She loved the way that he plundered her mouth like the centuries-old pirate she'd fantasized about him being, loved the way he took his pleasure but gave much more pleasure in return. The kiss was savage. It was primal. Yet it was still unbearably tender.

It was all things wonderful . . . and all things most terrifying.

And at that moment she was quite sure that it would be the death of her.

So Sean did the first thing that came to mind to save herself.

She slid her hands between them until they were flat against his belly and shoved him as hard and as far as she could.

She took a slow, ragged breath. "No."

FOUR

Dalton had felt as if he were halfway down the road to paradise when Sean's unexpected shove had sent him careening against a tall, scraggly pine.

He stood there for a good fifteen seconds, too, feeling the rough bark of the tree bite painfully into his upper back through the lightweight cotton of his T-shirt. He didn't mind the discomfort, though. He was much too busy trying to figure out what the hell had happened to him to care about anything else.

He stared at her in openmouthed confusion a moment longer, then shook his head.

"Wh-what?"

She met his gaze head-on. Her face was flushed with heat and her blue eyes smoldered with the same fire that still threatened to consume him body and soul . . . although from the rigidness of her stance, it was clear she was trying to pretend otherwise.

She squeezed her shaking hands into even shakier fists and stood her ground.

"I said . . . *no*."

She said it slowly, she said it firmly, and she said it just as succinctly and clearly as she'd said it the first damned time.

The fact that she'd said no wasn't the part that Dalton was having trouble comprehending.

It was the reason behind her decision to say it at all that he found unfathomable.

He drew a shaky breath and took a step toward her, his hand outstretched.

"Sean . . ."

A look closely resembling absolute terror shot across her face. She scrambled back out of his way as though the thought of being anywhere near him scared her half out of her wits.

He stopped, then raked his fingers through his hair. "Okay . . . then at least tell me why."

"You know why."

Her voice was so raw with emotion, he began to ache for her pain.

"No, I'm afraid I don't," he told her softly. "I don't have so much as a clue here. Why don't you explain it to me?"

"It's simple, Dalton," she said quietly. "We can't, that's all. Mixing business and pleasure . . . well, it's about as stupid as mixing alcohol and a road trip."

He swore bitterly. "Is that what this is about? You're worried about our *working* relationship? Dammit, Sean, get serious. We're both adults. We ought to be able to prevent our romantic involvement from interfering with the expedition."

"No, Dalton, *you* get serious. We don't have a romantic involvement right now, and we're not going to have one. I wouldn't have one with a member of my crew, and I sure as hell won't have one with an investor. Or even the grandson of an investor. The potential for complications is far too great."

He shoved his hands into the pockets of his khaki shorts in frustration.

"Sean, you know I want this expedition to succeed as much as you do. Hell, maybe more. In case you've forgotten, my grandfather has most of his life savings tied up in this thing. But—"

"And I've invested most of my life *period*," she countered, cutting him off. "That's why we have to stop this right now. We both have too much at stake to get swept away by our hormones."

He stared into her eyes for a long moment, searching for answers to questions he couldn't even begin to formulate into words.

"But I'm not willing to walk away from

what I feel for you," he said slowly. "Dammit, when I look at you . . ."

He squeezed his eyes closed and took a slow, deep breath. "When I look at you, the whole world seems to disappear," he said in wonder, opening his eyes. "I can't remember a time when I've had so many emotions tumbling through me at once. I don't know about you, but I figure that this could lead to something pretty damned fantastic."

He sought out her gaze. "I don't want to lose that feeling, Sean."

She seemed to stiffen her spine. "I'm afraid you'll have to," she said. "The timing is all wrong for us to have a fling."

"A fling?" He frowned at her. "Who the hell said anything about having a fling? I want a relationship with you, or at least a chance to see if we can have a relationship."

The look of terror returned to her eyes, only stronger this time.

"That . . . that is completely out of the question," she said hoarsely.

"It doesn't have to be if we don't let it. Look, Sean, I find you attractive. And I like you as a person. What's wrong with our getting to know each other better and seeing where this could lead?"

"Because it's pointless, that's why," she told him coldly. "It's not going to lead us anywhere."

He stared at her in stunned disbelief. "Are you telling me that you don't want me to touch you?"

She started to blush.

"I . . . no," she said.

"Are you telling me that you didn't enjoy that kiss we just shared as much as I did? Are you telling me that the thought of my making love to you right now doesn't half drive you out of your mind with desire?"

"I . . . dammit, Dalton," she said, her voice going rough around the edges. "I'm not saying any of that and you know it. This . . ." She took a deep breath. "It's not about whether or not I find you attractive or whether or not I want you to make love to me. We both know that the answer to those questions is yes."

"Then what the hell is it about?"

She fell silent.

An ugly possibility crossed his mind. "Oh, hell, you're not married, are you?" he asked. "Or involved in a serious relationship?"

"No," she said, looking shocked. "Absolutely not. I'm completely, totally single. And I want to stay that way."

She met his gaze. "Dalton, what I've been trying to say is that although I'm attracted to you, I feel that having a fling with a member of the expedition, especially with a representative of one of the investors, is a bad idea."

"But—"

"And a fling is all that we could ever have," she said, cutting him off. "Because I most emphatically am *not* interested in having a relationship with you or with anyone else. Not now," she said slowly. "Not ever. I don't want to settle down . . . or have babies . . . or anything else that even remotely resembles a commitment."

Now it was his turn to look shocked.

"Whoa." He raised his hands, palms outward. "I said I wanted to explore the possibility of a relationship. I never said anything about our having babies together. Making those kinds of long-term plans is a bit premature for us, don't you think?"

She shrugged. "But you're at least conceding the possibility of their existence," she told him. "I can't. You see, I don't want to get married. I don't want to have children. I don't want any long-term commitments. I have a satisfying career which allows me to travel, and no emotional entanglements to make me feel guilty about it. I like my life just the way it is."

"I see," he said, although he didn't believe her for a single, solitary moment.

Sean was a loving, giving woman who embraced life with her arms open wide. If ever there had been a woman cut out for all those emotional entanglements she seemed so hot to avoid, it was she.

Besides, he thought, staring at her for a moment longer, there was a hunger burning in her eyes when she talked about how much she didn't want those things. It was a hunger for something more emotionally fulfilling than hunting for pirate treasure too.

Then he remembered her description of her childhood and all the things that she'd wanted then but had never gotten. When you boiled it all down, she'd been searching all her life for emotional security.

He thought it was funny that that security was the one thing Sean now claimed she didn't need.

"I guess there's nothing much else for us to say then," he told her quietly.

She shrugged. "I guess not."

Dalton nodded curtly, then turned and started to make his way back down the path toward the camp.

He told himself to forget Sean, to forget his attraction to her and the memory of the kiss as well, although he knew in his soul that he probably never would be able to forget any of those things.

After all, telling yourself you shouldn't want something rarely ever squelched the desire. He smiled grimly. It was one of those little facts of life that someone should've probably explained to Sean a long time ago, but he imagined she'd discover it on her own.

Sooner or later, she'd have to find some way to feed that hunger inside her . . . or it would likely eat her alive.

Sean spent the remainder of the day working in the small clearing in front of the cavern.

She surveyed everything from the dense thickets of pine and vine-covered shrubs to the stands of cypress and tall marsh grass until her shoulders ached and her vision started to blur. She double-checked her previous calculations about the most probable locations for the site of LaRue's buried treasure chest, then triple-checked them with the same painstaking attention to detail that she'd used the first two times.

When she found herself considering doing yet a fourth such survey, she knew that she wasn't just being overly cautious about her mathematics. She was trying to avoid returning to camp and seeing Dalton again.

Sean scowled and returned the binoculars to their carrying case, which she then dropped into the canvas carryall. She started to dismantle the theodolite.

Unfortunately, Dalton would be staying at the camp and participating in the expedition for the next two months, and if she stayed out at the cavern any longer, she'd die from star-vation. She'd only had a half bowl of oatmeal and an apple for breakfast, and as for lunch, well, she'd skipped that altogether.

She shook her head in self-disgust. She was making a fool out of herself over him and she knew it. The fact that it had been a long time since a man had made her feel the way that Dalton Gregory did was beside the point. So what if she wanted him? So what if he wanted her? The pleasure they'd derive from giving in to the temptation didn't seem worth the risk, especially since he was the type of man who wanted more than a nice, uncompli-cated love affair.

He was the type who wanted far more than she could ever let herself give.

Sean zipped up the canvas bag and swung it onto her shoulders. As far as she could tell, she really only had one choice.

Since she couldn't give in to the feelings he evoked in her and get them—and him—out of her system, she'd have to ignore his too handsome face and his pirate smile, and she'd have to ignore the way they seemed to make her heart skip a beat and her body come alive, as well.

Then the memory of their kiss flashed into her mind, setting her body temperature rising a few degrees.

Yeah, she'd have to ignore the memories, too, she decided.

She'd have to block the feel of his firm chest pressing hard against hers, of his hands cupped so tenderly around her face, of the taste of his mouth and of his scent and of his voice and of his smile and . . .

Sean took a slow, ragged breath, then started back toward camp before the list of things she'd have to forget about Dalton grew any longer.

Ten minutes after she arrived back at camp, Sean realized her plan for simply ignoring her attraction to Dalton wasn't going to work.

In fact, she thought she'd probably have a better chance of ignoring one of the fundamental laws of nature—like gravity—than she would in ignoring one too-sexy-for-his-own-damned-good professor of American history.

Because as soon as her gaze locked with Dalton's, her heart began to pound and her pulse began to race and something closely resembling liquid fire began to flow through her veins.

Still, Sean refused to accept defeat. Instead she decided to intensify her efforts to ignore him.

All through dinner that night, she sat at

the long picnic table next to her brother, picking at her hamburger and trying to pretend with all her might that she wasn't aware of Dalton sitting across from her . . . that she wasn't acutely aware of the crackle of sexual chemistry that had seemed to spark between them when their fingers lightly brushed as he passed her a plate of hamburger buns . . . that she wasn't aware of the heat that swirled inside her each time he smiled at her, stealing her breath and making her body ache for his touch.

Ignoring him simply didn't work. She couldn't stop being aware of him any more than she could stop breathing and continue living. She promised herself that things would be easier in the morning, that all she really needed to fight her attraction to Dalton was a good night's rest.

But things weren't going to look any better in the morning, she decided later, because she couldn't get a good night's rest because she couldn't stop thinking about Dalton. She couldn't stop thinking about how he was lying in the tent just a few short feet away from hers, and she couldn't stop herself from speculating if he slept in the nude, just as she couldn't stop wondering what his reaction would be if she were to climb into his sleeping bag beside him and continue what they'd started back in the clearing near the cavern.

So, she decided to throw herself into her work, telling herself that once she started the actual excavation process, she would be so busy, she would have no time even to notice an attraction for him.

But all through the staking out of the first selected excavation site and all through the initial ground breaking of the site that followed, her attraction and hunger and need for Dalton grew until touching him and tasting him and loving him were all she seemed to be able to think about or care about.

On the morning of the third day, Sean finally was willing to accept defeat.

She couldn't ignore him, and she couldn't pretend to herself anymore.

She leaned her head against the shower stall and let the cool water rush over her.

The only thing she had to figure out now was exactly what she was going to do about it.

Dalton slid his hand up Sean's naked thigh, marveling at its exquisite softness. Her skin felt like hot satin. So smooth, yet sizzling to the touch. He slowly parted her legs, then eased his thumb into the folds of her slick feminine heat. He felt her shudder against him.

His heart pounding, he started to stroke

her, slowly at first, then gradually increasing his tempo until her eyes began to smolder and burn, until she started to writhe against his hand in near ecstasy, until she moaned his name and let her head fall back against the soft grass in wild abandon.

Lord, but she was beautiful, he thought. Her unbound hair was spread out around her like a copper-colored fan, and her face was flushed with passion.

He wanted to continue exploring her body, wanted to taste her and touch her until he'd gotten his fill, but Sean eased his hand away. She gave him a devilish sort of smile that set his soul on fire, then she pressed her fingertips against his shoulders and pushed him back to the ground, where she slowly straddled him, bringing those long legs of hers to rest against his hips.

She lowered herself onto him.

Heaven.

He groaned and thrust his hips up to meet hers. He glided his hands up her slender body to grasp her breasts, squeezing them, molding them in his palms, tweaking the nipples until they formed hard little peaks that he longed to taste as she moved against him. Faster. Harder. She gasped his name. Her voice was throaty, laced with huskiness, desire.

Then a bird began to squawk . . . and

Sean seemed to slip away like a puff of smoke from a campfire.

Hell.

Dalton reached out and tried to pull her back. He thought he almost had her, too, when the bird squawked again, only louder this time.

And Sean vanished.

Groaning in frustration, Dalton sat up and opened his eyes to find himself back in his sleeping bag, with a blackbird hopping around on the ground outside the closed flap of his tent.

"Damned bird," he muttered, collapsing back on his pillow.

It was the third dream it had interrupted in as many days.

Dalton lay there for a moment, his body hard with unreleased tension, his breathing shallow, his pulse racing . . . and the memory of Sean loving him still fresh in his mind.

He muttered a curse and kicked off the sleeping bag. This whole morning ritual of his was getting a little old, he decided, yanking on a pair of gym shorts. It was so old that he decided it was the last time he'd ever let it happen.

The way he figured it, he only had two options. He could either kill the bird to prevent any more early-morning serenades, or he could convince Sean that she was wrong about fighting their feelings.

He headed out of the tent to take a cold shower.

At the moment he wasn't even particular about which option he chose.

FIVE

Sean shut off the faucet, then squeezed the excess water from her hair before wrapping it securely in a towel. She felt a chill settle around her and shivered, then reached for a second towel and quickly dried herself off. It was amazing how frigid a nice, cool shower can quickly become, she thought wryly, briskly rubbing away the goose bumps popping up on her arms.

Especially once all thoughts of a certain American-history professor were finally, if only temporarily, stricken from her mind, she added with a smile.

Feeling overly pleased with herself just then for completing a task she had begun to feel was damn near impossible, she wrapped a large terry-cloth towel around her torso. Then she slipped her feet into a pair of plastic thonged sandals, opened the shower door, and started to make a run for her tent before she caught a case of double pneumonia.

All she succeeded in doing, however, was running full tilt into a bare-chested Dalton.

Sean let out a gasp and tried to pull back but couldn't. His hands were locked too tightly around her waist . . . and her cheek felt too damned good pressed against the warm, hard wall of his chest.

Worst of all, every last one of those erotically tinged images that she'd prided herself in finally suppressing moments before all came tumbling back.

Stronger than ever.

Images of Dalton's hands stroking her breasts and her abdomen and her hips until she softly moaned and arched her body toward him . . . images of Dalton's mouth melding with hers and of his tongue gliding over hers, pulling her deeper into a kiss that could liquefy her very bones . . . images of Dalton removing her clothes with an exquisite tenderness, then easing her back against a metal four-poster bed in the captain's quarters of an old pirate ship . . . images of Dalton then rising above her, naked and strong and oh so breathtakingly male.

Her heart started to pound. The muscles in her lower abdomen began to tighten.

Oh, dear God, not again.

The heat swept over her. It rose up from his chest and swirled around her until she couldn't breathe, until her knees began to shake and her vision started to blur. The heat shot out his fingertips, too, burning through the terry cloth until it scorched her skin.

The heat seemed to be all around her, but she felt it in her soul most of all.

And she knew he felt it too.

She could feel the rigid power of his arousal pressing against her abdomen as intensely as if he'd been completely unclothed, rather than wearing the lightweight gunmetal-gray gym shorts.

She shivered again, though not from the chill in the air this time.

She slowly looked up and met his gaze. She saw the unspoken need. The all-consuming desire. It burned as brightly in the shadows of his smoke-filled eyes as it burned inside her.

He swallowed hard and released her, then took an unsteady step backward.

"Ahhh, sorry," he muttered, raking a hand through his sleep-tousled hair.

His voice sounded rough, streaked with emotion, seared with want.

Her throat felt parched. "No. It . . . it's my fault," she said, knowing her own voice sounded as jagged around the edges as his.

And it *was* all her fault, too, she thought.

Every last bit of it. She was being ridiculous for trying to fight her feelings for Dalton, especially since she now knew she could never succeed in the attempt. She wanted him too damned much.

Besides, she thought, trying to rationalize her newly made decision, Dalton had been right. They were both adults. They ought to be able to handle any conflict of interest that might arise between the expedition and a passionate summer fling.

As for Dalton wanting more from her than just a summer fling . . .

A few seconds passed.

Sean slowly sighed like a person who'd held her breath for an eternity.

"Dalton," she said, "I've been thinking about what you said . . . about us."

He gave her a smile. It warmed someplace cold and dark inside her.

"Yes?" he murmured.

"These past few days have been driving me crazy," she admitted huskily. "I mean, I think about you all the time . . . and I think about that kiss."

She most especially had been thinking about that kiss, she quietly amended, feeling her cheeks begin to flame as its memory swept over her again.

His gaze didn't waver.

"And?" he asked.

"And . . . and maybe I was a little hasty earlier," she said. "Maybe a romantic involvement wouldn't have to cause problems for the expedition."

He didn't say anything.

"So, I was thinking," she went on. "Assuming you still feel the same attraction for me . . . well, maybe we should discuss acting upon some of these fantasies we've been having before we both go nuts."

His smile deepened, as did the heat in his gaze. He took a step closer.

"Sean . . ."

"Hey! You gonna use that shower, Dalton, or just stand outside it all morning?"

Ian's voice bellowed across the quiet campsite, like the boom of a cannon blast across the bridge of a sleeping ship.

Feeling herself blush straight down to her toes, Sean wrapped her arms across her chest as her brother joined them.

"Morning, sis," he said, giving her a quick peck on the cheek.

He was wearing a rumpled white T-shirt with more than its share of rips and holes and a pair of faded blue gym shorts. No shoes.

"Morning," she murmured back, hoping she didn't sound as flustered as she felt.

Ian nodded at Dalton. "Well? You going in or staying out?"

Dalton's smile turned into a near grin. "Sorry," he said. "I'll be out in a sec."

Then Dalton sought out Sean's gaze.

"About . . . what we were saying," he said softly.

The pounding in her heart seemed to grow louder, so much louder, she half expected her brother to phone for an emergency airlift out of fear she was going into cardiac arrest.

"Yes?" she murmured.

"I think . . . well, I think you've raised some valid points," Dalton said. "Why don't we take a walk later today and discuss them?"

"That would be great."

Dalton nodded, then moved past her with a soft whoosh of electrically charged air that sent a whole new round of goose bumps popping up on her arms . . . and a whole new wave of liquid heat coursing through her veins.

He stepped into the shower, glanced back, and gave her a grin, then closed the aluminum door behind him with a tiny metallic click.

Taking a deep breath, Sean turned around to find Ian staring at her with more than his usual amount of brotherly scrutiny.

He started to frown, then scratched his red beard-stubbled chin.

"Is, ah, something going on here I should know about?" he asked quietly.

She heard the squeak of the faucet as Dalton turned on the shower, followed by the hard spray of water hitting the aluminum sides of the stall. Then the tantalizing image of a fully unclothed Dalton swept over her.

She felt her blush deepen.

"No," she said hoarsely. "Wh . . . ?" She cleared her throat. "What makes you ask that?"

Ian shrugged. "I don't know. There's the way you're acting for one. And the way you've *been* acting since Dalton got here, for another."

"You're just imagining things," she told him.

He folded his arms against his chest and continued to stare.

"Maybe," he said. "Sometimes I try and tell myself that is exactly what I'm doing. Imagining things. Other times I tell myself that it's the stress of the expedition, the knowing that we're finally searching for LaRue's treasure after all the years of planning for it that's got you acting so . . . so unlike yourself."

She squeezed her hands into fists but still kept them wrapped around her chest.

"Dammit, Mudbug—"

"But then I start thinking about the way Dalton's been acting whenever he's around you," he said, cutting her off. "And the way that you two look at each other when you think no one's watching. All of these little things are inconsequential by themselves, but when you start adding them up . . . well, it becomes pretty obvious what's going on here."

He paused a moment, then smiled. "You're falling in love, sis. I think that's great."

"You think I'm—"

She sputtered a curse—one of her more particularly colorful epithets, in fact—then turned and stalked back toward her tent without another word.

"Hey," she heard Ian call after her. "Don't get so damned defensive! I said that I thought it was great, didn't I?"

Sean scowled, ducked inside her tent, then dropped its flap closed behind her.

Yeah, it was great, all right, she thought, undoing the towel around her torso. She was losing her sanity over a man, and her brother thought it was the neatest thing since microwave popcorn.

Then his precise words seemed to echo inside her head like an accusation.

You're falling in love, sis. . . .

Sean squeezed her eyes closed and let the damp towel fall to the ground.

"No!"

She repeated the word a few more times

until she decided it had finally been drummed into her subconscious, then opened her eyes, feeling somewhat better. She reached up, pulled off the towel from around her head, letting her damp hair tumble around her bare shoulders, and tossed the towel onto the ground next to the other one.

Ian was wrong, she reassured herself. He simply had to be.

Because the thought of what she felt for Dalton being anything more than simple lust was too damned frightening to contemplate.

Forty-five minutes later, after they had sat down at the camp's scarred picnic table for a quick breakfast of oatmeal and fresh fruit, Dalton realized that his plans for whisking Sean away for a private conversation—or anything else—would have to be put on hold.

Maybe even an indefinite one.

Because while Brian poured the coffee, Sean quietly announced that the excavation site at Area One would be abandoned, and the ground breaking at Area Two would begin immediately following breakfast.

Brian groaned; Ian's response was a tad more remonstrative. Dalton silently echoed the sentiment of each, although he was sure they were grumbling for entirely different reasons.

After having helped prepare Area One, Dalton knew what he and the rest of the team would be in for that day and the next. Setting up the new site would be slow, physically demanding work, with each team member working their own quarter share of a roped-off twenty-foot area. That wasn't the part that bothered him. It was knowing he wouldn't have a chance to be alone with Sean.

Although he would likely be able to see her all day long, they'd be involved in the kind of work that would leave precious little time for meal breaks, much less an opportunity to engage in the kind of intimate discussion that he felt they needed to have.

Still, Dalton knew the opening of Area Two was necessary. In fact, he'd been expecting the change in excavation sites for the past twenty-four hours. The preliminary soil analyses that Brian had performed earlier had proven inconclusive, so they'd had little choice but to do brief exploratory digs at each of the potential sites in the hope of finding a trace of the chest.

They'd spent three days working Area One with little to show for their efforts except blisters and aching backs from shoveling mud and water-soaked earth, and several brushes with sunstroke due to the humidity-laden temperatures. Dalton imagined they'd likely be spending another three days at Area Two, before moving on to the third. Using a small bulldozer would have been easier and faster, but it had been out of the question as far as Sean was concerned. The risk of damage or outright destruction of any artifacts LaRue might have left behind—as well as the potential loss of clues to the chest's precise location—was simply too high for her to take the chance.

Dalton agreed.

In the five short days he'd been with the expedition, he'd managed to get a good look at the way Setarip conducted its business, and he liked what he saw. Although they had yet to uncover any sign of a treasure chest, he was quite impressed with the way they ran their entire recovery operation.

He was also quite impressed with Sean herself.

He intended to tell her just how impressed once he got her alone, along with about a thousand other things such as how the glint of sunlight on her copper-colored hair stirred him, both body and soul . . . and how a single whiff of her perfume could send his pulse racing into the triple digits . . . or how he had lain awake nights thinking about her, only to fall asleep and continue his erotic fantasies in his dreams.

At around two-fifteen that afternoon, Dalton finally got his chance.

Ian and Brian returned to camp to pick up more scaffolding for the excavation site, leaving Dalton and Sean to clear the site of some of the dirt and mud their digging had unearthed.

Not wanting to waste a moment of the thirty or so minutes he expected Ian and Brian to be gone, Dalton pushed his dirt-laden wheelbarrow over to where Sean was building an earthen mound at the edge of the site next to a stand of scraggly pines.

He let his gaze slide over her, liking what he saw. Her once white T-shirt was streaked with dirt and clung to the hollow of her perspiration-dampened back. Her cutoff jeans were now more dusty brown than pale blue, and her long, shapely legs had more mud visible on them than lightly tanned skin.

In short, she looked like a woman who had spent the day doing hard manual labor in a muggy, water-soaked ditch, which was precisely what she was and what she'd been doing. To him, however, she was still more desirable than any lingerie-clad model reclining seductively against a red satin divan.

Because she was real.

Because she was Sean.

At that moment he realized that he wanted her more than he wanted another breath. But it was a want and a need for far more than her body.

Dalton swallowed hard.

The realization of how much more wrapped itself around his heart and squeezed.

She gave the pile of dirt and mud a not-so-gentle thump with the flat side of her shovel, then glanced over her shoulder at him.

"Hi," she said.

Her voice was the same soft Southern drawl of his fantasies . . . only in his fantasies she was telling him how much she craved his touch.

His heart started to pound. He felt his abdominal muscles begin to constrict. The need to reach out and touch her face, the need to stroke her cheeks and her lips and her chin until he'd stroked every inch of her was nearly overwhelming in its intensity.

"Hi," he said, tightening his grip on the warm metal handle of the wheelbarrow until his knuckles began to whiten.

She gave him a smile that was as warm and softly inviting as her voice had been, and he felt his hold on both his self-control and the handle of the wheelbarrow begin to loosen.

She motioned toward the mound of dirt. "Just go ahead and dump it."

He didn't move.

A few seconds passed.

"Well?" she asked, giving him a grin. "What are you waiting for, Dalton?"

What indeed?

Taking a deep breath, he walked over to her, grasped her shoulders, and pulled her to him until her slender body was pressed hard against his.

"I . . . Dalton?"

He slid his lips over hers, silencing her. She seemed to freeze for a heartbeat or so, then slowly melted against him like an ice cube on a hot summer day. He heard her drop the shovel, then felt her arms wind around his back and pull him closer.

After having fantasized about it for so long, he'd expected their second kiss to be primal and savage, that it would be the kind of kiss that would send them both exploding in a firestorm of sensual sparks that would melt their clothes and inhibitions in its white-hot flame. But it wasn't.

To the contrary, the kiss was soft and gentle. It was still filled with heart-pounding desire, but it was a desire tempered by caring. It was the kind of kiss a man could lose his soul in and not even care.

Dalton started to massage her shoulders, feeling her tense muscles begin to relax beneath his touch as the kiss deepened and grew. He wanted this . . . the kissing her, the holding her in his arms . . . to last forever. He wanted to taste her, leisurely, until he'd finally gotten his fill. Although something told him a century or two of kissing Sean would still not be enough to slake his hunger for her.

He moved his tongue against her lips, and she opened for him with a soft moan, then tightened her grip on his back, pulling him closer until his arousal pressed strong and hard against her lower abdomen. His tongue found hers, and they began a slow, erotic dance as old as time itself. Caressing, rubbing, sucking. Then the tenderness of the kiss gave way to the hunger of their desire, and the tempo of the dance of their tongues became more erotic still.

Sean groaned deep in her throat and took a step backward, pulling him with her, until she was braced against a pine. Then she slid her hands down his back to his buttocks and tugged him closer, where she began to rub herself against his arousal until he thought he'd lose his mind from the sheer want of her alone.

That's when he knew they had to stop. Now. That very instant. If he spent another second kissing her, he wouldn't give a damn about the likelihood of Ian and Brian's return in a few short minutes.

In another second spent kissing Sean, Dalton wouldn't give a damn about much of anything.

So he slowly pushed himself away.

He met her gaze. Her lips were swollen

with desire, her face was flushed, and her blue
eyes were smoldering with a passion so hot, it
could sear his very soul.

He gave her a smile.

"I've been wanting to do that all morning,
sweetheart," he murmured hoarsely. "Probably longer than that."

Hell, maybe even for most of his life, if he
were entirely honest with himself, although
until he'd met Sean he'd never known exactly
who it was he'd been dreaming of kissing.

She laughed, low and husky. He decided it
was the most beautiful sound he'd ever heard.

She slid her hands up his chest to rest on
his shoulders. "So have I," she murmured.
"Wanting you to do that, I mean."

She wound her arms around his neck and
gave him a hug. He surrendered to the feeling, marveling once again at how good, at how
unbelievably right, it felt to have her body
pressed against his.

"In fact, I want you to do it again," she
said, giving him a soft kiss on his chin.

The brush of her lips sent fire-laced shivers down his spine. His body began to ache
from the want of her, but he knew if he gave
in to the impulse to kiss her again, he
wouldn't be able to stop this time.

"I . . . don't . . . think that would be
such a good idea right now," he told her.

He gently unwound her arms and pushed her away.

"Timing, I mean," he said. "The others will be back soon, and we need to talk."

"Talk?"

"Yes. We need to finish what we were discussing back at camp."

"Hmm. Oh, that." She grinned and leaned against the tree.

"Yes, that," he said. "As I recall, you were telling me that you had reconsidered your earlier position about our getting involved."

She nodded.

"So . . ." he said slowly. "Does this mean you finally decided that we can handle any potential conflict between the expedition and a romance?"

She nodded again. "Provided we're both sensible about it, yes I think so."

"Sensible?" He frowned at her. "Define . . . *sensible*."

Her grin slowly faded. "Dalton, don't," she said softly. "I told you I wasn't looking for anything long-term. I meant that."

So why do you kiss the way you do? he wanted to ask but didn't.

Instead he just stared at her for a moment.

"Okay," he said. "So, exactly what are you proposing should happen between us?"

She held his gaze. "I'm proposing that we

explore this . . . attraction we have for each other in greater depth."

She spoke so matter-of-factly, she might have been discussing the opening of a new excavation site rather than the start of an intimate physical relationship.

"But we both have to agree that there is no way anything permanent can come of this," she said. "After all, you've got your teaching position at the University of Georgia, which is where you'll be headed in two months. Maybe even sooner, if Sammy's hip heals quickly. And I've got Setarip waiting for me back in Key Biscayne, which is where I'll be headed in the fall. That's assuming we don't find the chest, because if we do, then the LaRue Expedition is over . . . and we'll be going our separate ways a lot sooner than expected."

"I see," he murmured. "So . . . basically . . . you're suggesting that we have a nice, uncomplicated summer romance for as long as fate keeps us together?"

"Yes," she said, her gaze never wavering. "That's precisely what I'm suggesting."

He reached out and stroked her cheek with the pad of his thumb, gliding across the freckles, amazed at the exquisite softness of her skin. He felt her draw in an unsteady breath.

"And what if the summer isn't enough for

us, Sean?" he asked. "What if we both decide that we need more? What then, sweetheart?"

"That . . . that won't happen," she told him. Her voice trembled slightly.

He slid his thumb over the curve of her mouth. "Are you sure?"

"I . . . yes," she said. "I'm sure. It's the only alternative we have."

He frowned. "But it's not," he told her softly. "We have a chance for a genuine relationship here. One that doesn't have to end once the summer is over unless we wanted it to."

"No!"

She pushed away his hand and seemed to stiffen her spine like a soldier coming to full attention.

"Dalton, I'm sorry," she said huskily. "But this is a nonnegotiable point. I don't want anything long-term. You can either agree to that, or we forget the entire thing. The choice is yours."

He held her gaze, watching the war of emotions that played across her face. He felt something tighten inside him.

"Sean . . ."

Dalton took a deep breath and changed his mind. It was pointless to continue arguing with someone who refused to see the truth.

"Okay," he told her wearily. "We'll have it

your way. No strings. No long-term involvements. Just an uncomplicated summer fling."

"Great," she said.

Then the sound of laughter, of movement from the path leading back to camp, floated toward them. Dalton gave her a short nod, then turned back to his wheelbarrow and began to dump out the load of dirt.

Regardless of what Sean said, though, he knew in his soul that she wanted more than just a casual fling. He could sense it in the way she talked about it, feel it in the way she kissed.

Sooner or later, he figured she'd have to realize it too.

He started to push the empty wheelbarrow back to his section of the excavation.

All Dalton could do was wait . . . and hope that the realization came before she succeeded in breaking his heart into a million or so unsalvageable pieces.

Later that night, Sean sat in her darkened tent, with her knees pulled up to her chest, staring at the luminescent numbers on her travel clock, watching the minutes tick slowly by.

"Coward," she whispered.

And she was one too.

She'd agreed to meet Dalton in his tent

after everyone had gone to sleep, but the camp had been quiet for nearly an hour, and she still hadn't moved so much as a muscle.

At first, she'd tried to tell herself that she was being cautious, that discretion was always the wisest course to take whenever dealing with a case of overactive hormones. But that excuse of hers was beginning to wear more than a little thin.

Brian's snores had been softly echoing through the campsite for the past forty-five minutes. As for Ian . . . well, he'd turned the light out in his tent about thirty minutes before, and if she knew her baby brother, he'd been asleep five minutes later.

So just what, she asked herself in mounting frustration, was she waiting for?

Then the image of Dalton flashed into her mind . . . of Dalton's pirate smile, then of his lips gently nuzzling her neck, of his hands slowly stroking her body, of his voice whispering sweet promises of their future together into her ear.

Her stomach did a somersault, and she felt her heart begin to pound.

Oh, great, she thought in self-derision. Just great.

From the way she was acting, a person would think she was some lovestruck teenager about to lose her virginity. She and Dalton were both adults, and they both made an adult decision to have a mutually satisfying, no-strings-attached affair.

An affair was all they could ever have together, she reminded herself forcefully, regardless of what Dalton might try to tell her, and regardless, too, of all the romantic nonsense that she might even be persuaded to start telling herself while sitting alone in her tent late at night, fantasizing about the man.

After all, that kind of happily-ever-after silliness was little more than a fairy tale, and a dangerous one at that—especially if you allowed yourself to be caught up in all of its accompanying emotional dependency.

Fortunately, Sean knew better than to let herself do that. She'd learned a long time ago that you couldn't count on anyone but yourself.

It had been a hard lesson that she doubted she would ever forget.

Telling herself that she'd waited long enough for the entire state of Florida to fall asleep—and that she either needed to follow through on her libidinous plans for Dalton or completely put both them and him from her mind—Sean scrambled to her feet and walked out of the tent into the clearing.

She glanced around.

A full moon hung overhead. The only sound for miles was the occasional chirp of a cricket and the croak of a frog. There were no rustlings of the nearby underbrush by nocturnal predators, large or small. Even the owls seemed to have fallen asleep.

She looked around her again before cautiously making her way to Dalton's tent. Then she paused just outside it.

A second passed.

Then two.

Finally, Sean took a deep breath, opened the flap, and walked inside the tent.

"Dalton?" she softly called.

A click followed, and the tent was flooded with light from his battery-operated lamp.

He gave her a smile so warm and inviting it could have melted her bones, and it damn near did, since her knees felt suddenly wobbly, as though they might not be able to carry her own weight.

Soon, everything else seemed to disappear from view except his face . . . and the realization of how much she truly did want him.

"Hi, sweetheart," he murmured huskily.

She let the flap fall closed behind her and returned his smile.

"Hi," she murmured back.

SIX

Dalton decided he'd never seen anything more beautiful than the way Sean looked standing inside the opening of his tent.

It wasn't that she'd altered her normal appearance. Except for the shower she'd taken before dinner, which washed away the dirt and grime she'd accumulated at the excavation site, she looked much the same as she had all day—work boots, denim cutoff jeans, scoop-necked tee in a soft shade of lavender with a touch of darker-colored lace near her cleavage.

No, her soul-stirring beauty came from the soft flush that colored her cheeks and the gentle, almost nervous smile she was offering him. She'd also undone her hair from its loose French braid. It tumbled around her shoulders in long silken waves that were the deep, rich color of rubies . . . rubies priceless enough to rival any that Jackson LaRue may have kept in the treasure trove the expedition was now searching for.

Only Dalton suspected that Sean Kilpatrick was a treasure worth far more than all the jewels any pirate chest could contain.

He felt that muscle stretch a bit tighter around his heart.

"I, ah, was beginning to think you wouldn't show," he told her huskily.

She walked toward him and sat down on the ground next to the sleeping bag.

"I just wanted to make certain everyone was asleep," she said.

There was a tremor so slight to her voice, he thought he could have imagined it.

He gave her another smile and reached for her hand. It felt like ice. He slowly began to rub it.

"I'd hoped I could scrounge us up a bottle of wine," he said, dropping his voice lower. "But I checked the food locker and there wasn't any."

She gave him a blank look. "Wine?"

He nodded. "I thought we could toast ourselves with a glass or two in the moonlight," he said. "A moment like this needs something special to mark the occasion, don't you think?"

He lifted her hand and brushed his lips over her knuckles.

"Since there was no wine," he went on, "I decided to improvise. The next best thing for commemorating any occasion is chocolate. *That* I could find. Someone had stashed a half-eaten bag of chocolate-chip cookies in the back of the cupboard. They may be stale, but they're all we've got."

She laughed.

Again, he was reminded of both the tinkle of crystal wind chimes in a summer breeze and the power of the wind itself.

The sound sent delicious shivers tumbling down his spine. He felt his body begin to harden.

"I'm surprised there were any cookies left," she told him. "Ian usually demolishes the entire bag the first day out."

Dalton gave her hand another squeeze, then reached for the cookies. He opened the bag and passed it to her.

"Thanks," she murmured, and took a cookie.

He took one for himself and set the bag back on the ground.

"Here's to us," he said, touching the tip of his cookie to hers.

She smiled. "To us," she echoed, and returned the toast. She bit into her cookie and slowly chewed. "Hmm . . . these are good."

They ate their cookies then, neither saying anything for a moment.

"Nervous?" he asked her. He reached for the bag and passed it to her.

She flushed. "A little."

She took out another cookie and bit into it.

He grinned. "Me too," he confessed. He reached for her hand again.

"You know, sweetheart," he said, "we don't have to rush into anything we're not ready for. Saying we want to have an affair and then actually following through on it are two different things."

She met his gaze, then moved her hand until their palms were flat against each other.

"I know," she said, interlocking their fingers.

She held out her cookie with her other hand and offered him a bite. He took it and slowly chewed.

Suddenly, stale, store-bought chocolate-chip cookies tasted like ambrosia.

She popped the rest of the cookie into her mouth.

"I mean," he went on, "it's perfectly okay if you decide that you don't want anything to happen between us tonight. I'll be a little disappointed, of course, but I'll understand."

She slid her fingertips across his mouth, stopping him.

He felt his abdominal muscles start to spasm.

"It's okay," she told him softly. "I'm sure."

"Yeah?" he asked huskily.

She grinned, then reached over and clicked off the lantern, sending the tent into semidarkness.

"Yeah," she said.

Then she kissed him. Slowly. Deeply. She gave him the kind of a kiss that was designed to demonstrate just how certain she was of wanting him . . . and of wanting this . . . and she succeeded on both counts.

It was amazing, he thought, leaning in to her. It was amazing how a single kiss could ignite him, both body and spirit, making him burn from a heat unlike any he'd ever experienced before.

It was amazing how the feel of her lips against his could turn his blood to liquid fire and make his heart thud so wildly against his chest that he thought it might explode from the pressure.

She curled her fingers around the back of his head, lightly ruffling his hair, and pulled him closer. Her tongue slid into his mouth with the ease of longtime lovers and sought out his, then slowly began to stroke it with the tip of hers.

Teasing.

Tormenting.

But with the promise of more fulfillment than any man could dream possible.

He groaned deep in his throat, tightened his grip on her hand, and pulled her to him until he could feel the soft curves of her breasts crushed against his chest, until the soft seductive scent of her perfume filled his lungs . . . maybe even a bit of his soul too. Then he let himself taste her.

She tasted as sweet as the chocolate-chip cookies they'd just shared . . . and far more intoxicating than the wine he'd hoped they could have drunk together.

She was like a drug, he decided, feeling his small section of the world begin to tilt. One kiss and she became an instant addiction for which there was no cure and no relief from its symptoms, save another kiss . . . and then another after that . . . followed by an endless number of kisses. The truth was, he could kiss her forever and still wouldn't get enough of her, of her touch, of her mouth, or of her tongue gliding around his.

Dalton couldn't think of a better way to spend all eternity than kissing Sean and having her return each of his kisses with the same frenzied need that he felt for her.

She slowly released her hand from his and slid her palm up his chest, scorching through the lightweight cotton of his T-shirt to sear his skin. She cupped his beard-stubbled chin and pulled him closer, then she intensified the kiss, slowly building the rhythm of the strokes of her tongue against his until he shuddered.

He wanted to touch her, had to touch her or else he feared he'd likely go insane from the unfulfilled need of touching her.

He stroked her hair first, marveling at how it felt like spun silk, letting each long strand run between his fingers as the kiss deepened and grew. He released her hair and eased his hands down her face, stroking her cheeks, then her neck and her shoulders, until he reached the swell of her breasts through her shirt.

He gave her breasts a proprietary squeeze, feeling a wave of sensual heat wash over him as his hands wrapped around them, loving the way they seemed to mold against his palms just as they had in his dreams. Then he slipped a hand inside the neck of her tee until he could feel the lacy edge of her bra . . . and the heat of her fevered bare skin.

His pulse started to race. His abdominal muscles began to constrict.

He stroked her breasts through the bra, first one, then the other, lovingly, tenderly, before giving each nipple a playful pinch with his thumb and forefinger, taking delight in the way they hardened into two tiny nubs, and taking pleasure, too, in the soft moan that rumbled low in her throat.

"I . . . used to think you were trying to drive me crazy," she murmured hoarsely against his mouth. "Now I know that you are."

He gave a low and husky laugh. "I'm just getting started, sweetheart," he promised her.

And he was.

He wanted to make the night last forever, wanted to love her as no man had ever loved her before. He wanted to watch her face as her climax overtook her, again and again. He wanted to imprint the memory of his touch on her for a lifetime and more.

Most of all, though, he wanted to make her realize that she needed more than some short-term, hotter-than-sin, no-expectations-beyond-the-present kind of fling with him. He wanted to make her realize that what she really needed was a commitment, the kind that could last the rest of their lives.

The kind that he knew he needed so desperately from her.

At that moment Dalton realized that he was in love with Sean. He knew it in his bones and muscles and sinews. He knew in the hot rush of blood flowing through his veins that seemed to sing her name. He knew it in the way his skin sizzled from her touch and in the way his body responded to hers as though they had made love together for years instead of this once.

Hell, he thought in sudden amazement as the flames of desire began to lick hotter around him. He'd probably been in love with her since the moment he'd first seen her standing in the middle of the expedition's campsite, covered with mud and grease as she worked on the generator. A hundred years from now, he'd probably still be in love with her too.

It was as though there were an undefinable quality about Sean Kilpatrick that filled an empty spot somewhere deep inside him. It was a feeling of such total completeness that now that he'd finally found it, he didn't think he could ever let himself lose it again. No matter how much Sean might try to fight against it. He couldn't bear to lose her.

Not now.

Not ever.

Moaning her name, Dalton sought out her lips again, thrusting his tongue inside her mouth to taste its sweetness once more. Her only response was to wind her arms around his back, hugging him closer.

Wanting more, needing more than he could ever put into words, he pulled back slightly until he could maneuver his knee between her legs. Then he started to rub himself against her with an ever-increasing rhythm, hoping to make the liquid heat coil tighter and hotter inside her body the way it was doing in his own.

She groaned, low and deep and primal, and clutched him tighter.

His erection began to press painfully against his khaki shorts, and he longed to strip off their clothes, push her down, and thrust himself deep inside her—but he fought the urge.

Soon, he told himself. Soon, he could concentrate on his own pleasure.

For now, though, he wanted to take her on an erotic journey of the senses.

For now, he wanted to stake his claim on her body, and maybe even her heart. Then they could both bask in the heat of their shared afterglow.

He broke off the kiss, grabbed the sides of her shirt in his hands, and gently tugged it out of the waistband of her denim shorts. He slid it up her body, exposing the pale skin of her abdomen and the full roundness of her breasts encased in their lacy white bra.

The soft floral scent of her perfume rose up and floated around him. He took a deep breath, inhaling the sweet fragrance until he felt as though he were coming dangerously close to sensory overload.

His mouth went dry. His body began to ache from the unrelenting tension.

Sean struggled to sit and helped him tug off the T-shirt, which he then dropped onto the ground next to the sleeping bag. Then he fumbled with the metal hooks of her bra, finally got them undone, and let her breasts fall free and unencumbered.

They were perfect, he decided. Not too large. Not too small. The ideal size to fit in the palms of his hands.

"You're . . . so . . . beautiful," he whispered softly, feeling a little awestruck.

She was far more beautiful than she'd even been in his wildest fantasies.

"I love it when you talk utter nonsense to me," she said huskily. "Tell me more."

He slid the straps of the bra down her shoulders, then tossed it to lie over her shirt.

"I'd rather have you talk to me," he said. "Tell me what you want, sweetheart . . . tell me what you need for me to do right now more than anything."

"Hmm," she murmured. "Let . . . me think."

He leaned down and kissed the bony ridge between her breasts. Her skin was hot, feverish. He felt her shiver, then felt the rustle of her fingers weaving through his hair. He raked the tip of his tongue down the same path along her chest, loving the way she took a sharp intake of breath and how her fingers tightened in his hair.

"Don't think, Sean," he told her. "Feel."

He palmed her breasts, gently rubbing the tips of his thumbs across her nipples until they tightened into hardened nubs again.

"Just tell me what you feel, sweetheart."

"I . . . oh, I feel like I'm melting," she said. "I like the way you touch me, Dalton."

Her voice was laced with the same hunger that was coursing through his veins.

"And I like the way you kiss me too," she added. "Like a pirate . . . so bold, so brash . . . so good."

"And how many pirates have you kissed?" he teased.

"Counting this week?" she asked.

"Hmm . . . yes."

He licked his tongue over each of her hardened nipples before settling his mouth around one and starting to suck while gently tweaking the other between his thumb and forefinger.

"Well, you . . . you'd be my first, actually," she said huskily.

He intended to be her last too.

"Still a woman has a way of knowing these things," she told him, speaking slowly as though she were trying to keep her voice steady. "Look at all of those old drawings of Jackson LaRue, at that knowing smile each artist seemed to capture. You can tell that he—"

He switched breasts. She drew a sharp intake of breath, held it a moment, then slowly exhaled.

"You can just tell that LaRue must have been a world-class kisser," she went on, sounding more husky still. "Elizabeth Martene's journal even backs up my theory. She said the brush of his lips on her hand made her swoon. You . . . you do that to me, Dalton," she whispered softly. "You do that and more."

"Hmm," he murmured. "I make you swoon, huh? I think I like that."

He increased the pressure of his knee against her groin, making his thrusts more erotic, more sensual, until he could feel the need, the hunger burning through her.

"I . . . oh, Dalton!"

She shuddered against him.

She was close, he thought with satisfaction. So close he could feel it.

He raised his head. Her face was cast in shadows, but he could still see the hunger and the need and the sweet torment all burning bright in her fever-streaked gaze.

"Too . . . much?" he asked huskily.

"Not . . . nearly . . . enough," she told him, tightening her hold on his shoulders.

Her voice sounded frayed around the edges, as though she were slowly unraveling from the inside out.

He decided that he loved her this way. He loved her wild with desire, wanton and free, just as a pirate's life partner should have been. But as good as it was, he still wanted more.

He wanted to make her spiral out of control and watch her face as it happened.

He moved his knee and reached for the zipper on her denim shorts. He slid it down, then eased his hand inside to touch her. He could feel her feminine heat through her cotton panties. It almost scorched his fingertips. He stroked her, moving with light feather touches that made her slowly squirm.

Then he slipped his hand into her panties and sought out the mound of soft curls at the base of her thighs, searching for the right spot. He felt her tense when his fingers brushed against her throbbing button of desire, and he smiled. He began to massage her with his thumbs, until the slow squirm became more of an uncontrollable writhe of pure, unadulterated ecstasy.

He raised his head to watch her face.

"Does it feel good, Sean?" he whispered, his voice raw with need. He increased the tempo of his strokes. "Tell me, sweetheart. I need to know."

Her hips began to move faster in rhythm with his strokes.

"I . . . oh, yes!"

He slowed the rubbing of his thumb

against her and her body's movement slowed in response.

"Good," he told her. "Am I making you swoon yet, sweetheart?"

"I . . . swoon, hell! I'll be lucky if you don't flat out kill me."

He grinned.

"Sorry, but I can't seem to help myself," he told her. "You see, I like touching you . . . and kissing you. In fact, I intend to spend the rest of the night doing a combination of both."

And if he had his way, that was how he'd like them to spend the rest of their lives too.

"I . . ." She moaned again. "Maybe I should have warned you," she said, shuddering again. "It's . . . been a long . . . time . . . for me."

"It's been a long time for me too," he said.

And it had never felt this good, this unbelievably right before.

"But like I told you before, sweetheart, we've got all night. So let yourself go."

"I . . ."

"I want to hear you come, Sean," he whispered, stroking her harder. "Come for me, baby. Right now."

She moaned again, the sound so low and deep, it could have been pulled from the depths of her soul, and she arched herself toward his hand.

"That's it," he murmured. "Just like that. Come for me."

He intensified his strokes and reached for her mouth, needing the feel of her lips against his and of her tongue sliding over his and of her hips moving against his hand as she came apart for him. This was for her, all for her, but it was for him as well, because he needed to know that she wanted him, that she needed him as desperately as she did her next breath.

And when her moans became steadily louder and her body started to buck against his hand and she returned his kisses with a wild abandon that nearly stole his soul, he continued to touch her as he let her ride it out, loving the knowledge that he was the one, the only one, who could make her feel this way.

Sean decided that she had never felt so alive, so utterly energized as she did at that precise moment. It was as if every cell of her body had been roused from a deep slumber and was now screaming with sheer joy at its sudden awakening.

Her heart thudded wildly, her skin tingled. In short, she felt . . . glorious.

She struggled to sit up.

Her gaze locked with Dalton's.

He gave her a grin that was vintage pirate. Sexy. Devilish.

And it held more than a trace of a self-congratulation at the moment, too, as though he were terribly pleased with himself.

Perhaps a little too pleased to suit her tastes.

She blushed.

"I love the way you sound when you come," he told her huskily.

The sensual quality of his low, deep voice, more than his actual words, sent dozens of white-hot tremors tumbling around her.

Her mouth went dry. The muscles in her lower abdomen began to constrict.

"I, ah, didn't realize that I'd said anything," she told him.

But then, everything had happened to her so quickly, it was no wonder she didn't remember talking. The rush of sensations had been like tumbling over the side of a tall waterfall in a softly cushioned crate: wild, frenzied, but unbelievably safe.

"Hmm," he told her. "Oh, you were quite vocal."

She felt her blush intensify.

Then he traced a slow outline on one of her breasts. She felt her nipple begin to harden and the liquid heat start to flow through her veins again.

"I thought it was great," he said, his voice

raw with need and suppressed desire. "A man likes to know when he's pleasing his woman."

His woman.

He'd said it so casually, as if it were a fact few would dare to question.

What was more, she decided she liked hearing him say it. She liked the way he'd staked ownership over her, even if she knew it was only his hormones talking.

"Hmm . . . well, you did," she said. "Pleased me, I mean."

"Is that so?" he murmured.

He raised his other hand and began to palm both breasts, then he gave each nipple a gentle tweak between his thumb and forefinger that sent shock waves of pleasure shuddering through her.

"Yes," she said slowly. "It was wonderful. *You* were wonderful. Now, however, I think it's time I returned the favor."

She reached for the hem of his cotton T-shirt and tugged upward, loving the smooth hardness of his bare skin, loving the soft rustle of his dark brown chest hair beneath her fingertips.

"I want to please you, Dalton," she whispered hoarsely. "I want to hear you come for me."

"Oh, trust me, baby," he told her in a voice just as hoarse. "You will."

He helped her remove his shirt, which she

then tossed aside. It landed on top of the bag of chocolate-chip cookies next to the lantern.

"Have I told you that I like the way your body feels?" she asked.

She slowly touched him, smoothing her hands over his shoulders, over the well-defined muscles of his arms, wanting to caress and stroke every last inch of him.

"So hard . . . so strong," she murmured. "I don't think I could ever get tired of touching you."

He sighed with contentment and settled back against the sleeping bag.

"That's good," he murmured. "Because my body likes the way you touch it."

"Really?"

She slid her hand over his crotch and began to massage him through his khaki shorts.

"Especially when I do this?" she asked.

He moaned, soft and low, and thrust himself up against her palm.

He felt so hard, she thought with amazement. Primed for release. Knowing that he'd put aside his own needs for the sake of hers touched her in a way she didn't quite understand.

She only knew that she wanted to return the pleasure he'd shown her a hundredfold.

"So what other things does your body like besides the way I'm touching you?" she whispered.

"Oh . . . this is good," he told her. "But I'm always open for suggestions."

She caressed him for a moment longer, then pulled away. She untied the laces of her work boots, pried both them and her thick socks off, and set them aside. Then she went to work on the laces of his sneakers. Once untied, she slowly removed the shoes and dropped them next to her boots. Then she rolled down his white socks as well.

She glided her hands over his feet, lightly raking her nails along his soles, then gently massaging his toes and feet until he sighed. She ran her hands up his leanly muscled calves, feeling the soft dark hair bristle beneath her fingertips, to rest against his hips.

"What would you like me to do to you right at this moment?" she asked, repeating the question he'd demanded of her not too long before.

His gaze locked with hers.

"Other than your loving me, sweetheart?" he asked hoarsely.

Hunger, need blazed in the shadowed depths of his eyes, along with another emotion she told herself that she would be better off not thinking about.

"Because I honestly can't think of a single thing that I need more from you than that," he went on. "Just . . . love me, Sean. That's all I need . . . that's all I could ever want."

She felt something tighten inside her. "Dalton . . ."

"But if you prefer," he went on, "I could tell you what I've been dreaming about our doing every night for nearly a week now."

"Oh?"

She continued to massage him through his shorts, loving the way he moved against her palm.

"Wild dreams," he said, "of an even wilder heaven that we found together."

"Hmm," she murmured. "Maybe you'd better tell me about them."

He reached out and stroked her breasts again, squeezing her nipples between his thumbs and forefingers until she shuddered, until a surge of sensual heat swirled around her, making her body tingle and setting her nerve endings deliciously aflame.

Liquid heat began to pool in her lower abdomen. Her body began to ache to feel him inside her.

He met her gaze. Held it.

"You're on top of me," he said. His voice sounded rough with emotion. "You're riding me. Hard. With those long legs of yours straddling my hips."

Her heart started to pound. She slipped her hand inside the waistband of his shorts and slid her palm around the length of his arousal. He felt like velvet heat. She stroked him again, feeling him grow stronger, harder with each massage of her hand.

He shuddered.

"Sean . . . baby."

She knew without his saying anything that he was close to rocketing out of control, so she eased her hand away. Then she tugged on his shorts, pulling them and his briefs down his hips. He raised himself slightly and helped her take off his clothes.

She quickly slid out of her own shorts and panties, then slowly straddled his hips until his arousal rested against her abdomen.

"In this dream you've been having about me, sweetheart," she murmured huskily, using the same endearment he'd used on her. "Are we positioned something like this?"

She moved herself against him.

He only groaned and wrapped his fingers around her hips and shuddered against her again.

"Condoms," he muttered hoarsely. "Back of my shorts pocket."

She reached behind her for the shorts and fished out the gold foil packet. She handed it to him. He quickly tore it open. He started to put on the condom, then she slipped her fingers over his hand and stopped him.

He glanced up and met her gaze, looking confused. She gave him a smile, then helped him slowly roll the latex into place over his arousal.

Nothing had ever felt so intimate or so unbearably sensual.

"You didn't answer my question," she reminded him huskily.

He drew in a sharp breath, held it for a moment, then slowly exhaled.

"I want you, Sean," he whispered. "Now."

Then he grasped her hips and pulled her closer, until his shaft slowly rubbed against her own slick feminine heat.

"I want you too," she whispered back. "But I have to know. Is this the way it happened when you dreamed about me?"

More than anything, she wanted to make that fantasy come true for him.

Then she raised herself up and eased down onto the hard length of him, moving slowly and steadily until he was fully inside her.

"Yes, baby," he whispered, closing his eyes as though he were in ecstasy. "It . . . it was just like this."

She shuddered against him.

"Good," she murmured.

Then she raised herself up and slid down on him again, pulling him deeper inside her this time. She glided her hands over his chest, loving its heat and its hardness, and started to move against him, searching for their natural rhythm.

He moaned, then raised his hips and pulled hers down harder, driving himself deeper inside her.

She moaned in reply, then slowly arched her back, feeling more wanton and free than she had ever felt before.

He was right, she thought with amazement.

This was a wild heaven.

"Sean . . ."

His voice was racked with need.

"I need to kiss you," he whispered.

Suddenly she needed to kiss him too.

She lowered her head and met his mouth. His kiss was wild, frantic, fueled by the fever that burned through them both.

She could feel the fireburst growing within her again. It was more powerful than the last had been, more powerful than she could have ever imagined possible. She continued to move with him, though, letting the fireburst's intensity slowly build, pulling him deeper, wanting him closer, squeezing him tighter with the walls of her body, knowing instinctively that he needed it too.

Then he groaned and thrust himself up, whispering her name against her mouth with such need and such caring that it triggered her own release . . . and she shuddered against him as well, calling out his name.

Time passed.

Sean just lay atop Dalton, with his arms wrapped around her back, feeling him still locked inside her and her heart thudding so loudly in her chest, it was all that she could hear. Her breathing was ragged and shallow and unsteady, just as his was, and her skin still sizzled from his touch. She wasn't sure if she wanted to move, even if she had the strength.

Then she slowly raised her head and met his gaze.

"That . . . was some dream you've been having about us, Dalton," she told him huskily.

He gave her a warm and tender smile, then cupped her face in his hands.

"Hmm," he murmured. "Yes, it was."

He brushed his lips over hers . . . and the heat began to build inside her again.

"Give me about ten minutes, sweetheart," he said, "and we'll start on one of yours."

SEVEN

Shortly after dawn, the blackbird started its morning wake-up squawk from outside Dalton's tent.

Dalton muttered a curse but didn't open his eyes. He was enjoying his sleep too much to worry about a bird on a suicide mission.

He'd had another one of his dreams about Sean, only this one had been much more vivid than all the others combined. It had been so vivid that the delectable images were still tumbling through his sleep-permeated brain . . . images of her naked, with her red hair spilling around her bare, slightly freckled shoulders and of the rich, creamy mounds of her breasts molding themselves against his hands . . . images of her long legs wrapped tightly around his hips as he plunged himself deep into her . . . images of her warm, throaty moans as he sent her spiraling deliciously out of control into another orgasm.

Dalton sighed. As dreams went, he'd have to classify this one as an instant classic.

Smiling softly, he rolled onto his side only to hear the unmistakable crunch of the empty bag of chocolate-chip cookies . . . cookies that he distinctly remembered he and Sean having demolished in his dream after one of their marathon bouts of lovemaking.

He came immediately awake.

It hadn't been a dream, he thought in wonder. It had been real. Him. Sean. Together. Sharing a white-hot passion that still took his breath away.

He let the information sink in for a moment and started to grin.

"Morning, sweetheart," he murmured, rolling over to give her a kiss.

Only she wasn't there.

He glanced around the empty tent.

She'd vanished as completely in real life as she had in his erotic dreams about her.

He had no idea how long she'd been gone, either. She could have slipped out of his arms a few moments before, or she could have left hours earlier, after he'd fallen asleep holding her close.

"Damn," he muttered.

Her leaving was more than just a blow to his male ego—which, after the strokes she'd given it during the night, could withstand a few direct hits by mortar fire and still not falter.

No, her leaving cut much deeper than pride. It sliced into his soul. She'd been making a statement, issuing an unpleasant reminder.

Sean wanted him to know that she'd been dead-cold serious about her resolve not to become emotionally involved with him.

He took a deep breath and raked his fingers through his hair.

Fortunately, he'd been just as serious about making her realize otherwise.

The blackbird squawked again, and Dalton glanced toward the open flap of the tent. The bird hopped a step closer then cocked its head to one side and stared at him. "Now what?" it seemed to ask.

Now what, indeed?

Dalton kicked off the unzipped sleeping bag they'd been using as a blanket. He reached for his gym shorts and yanked them on. The bird turned and flew off into the marsh with a loud flapping of its wings.

He needed to think, Dalton told himself. He also needed some coffee and a cold shower, which were probably an even bigger priority at the moment. It would likely be another long, exhausting day at the excavation site and he'd gotten maybe a total of two hours sleep all night.

As for what he was going to do about Sean . . .

Dalton sighed.

He'd start with the shower.

Then he'd figure out the rest as he went along.

Sean lifted the lid to the laundry hamper located just outside the communal showers and dropped in her panties and bra, then closed it. She stepped into the shower stall and pulled the metal door shut behind her.

Her muscles felt tight and achy and sore but all in a decidedly good way.

Almost too good, she thought as the memories swept over her.

Dalton had more than kept his promise of spending the night touching and kissing her. Making love with him had been wild, wonderful, erotic . . . yet it had all been underscored with a much deeper emotion than good old-fashioned lust.

It had been the kind of emotion that she didn't need in her life.

Sean groaned.

Why had she ever agreed to have an affair with Dalton? she asked herself.

True, he made her body come alive each

time he looked at her. But he had also made little secret of the fact that he wanted more than just a fling with her. Even though he'd also told her that he was willing to accept her terms for their romantic involvement, she wasn't sure if she could believe him.

After all, men like Dalton didn't believe in flings. Men like Dalton were dependable and good and loving, traits he seemed to have in overabundance. He was a tender pirate who could sweep a woman off her feet one moment with heart-pounding kisses, then hold her so lovingly the next, she felt nothing else mattered to him in the entire universe except her.

Worst of all, men like Dalton represented the future and all things wonderful that could happen between a man and a woman.

Sean had always considered that kind of romantic nonsense to be . . . well, romantic nonsense.

Until now.

Because each time Dalton touched her, each time he kissed her, she found that it was becoming easier and easier to believe in any number of adult fairy tales.

Scowling, she pointed the shower nozzle away from her face, then turned it on full blast, letting its cool spray hit the side of the shower stall. She pulled off her T-shirt and slipped out of her shorts, then cautiously opened the metal door wide enough for her to place them on top of the lid to the laundry hamper.

She was pulling her arm back inside the shower when she felt five warm fingers wrap around her hand and gently squeeze.

She gasped.

The shower door slowly opened and, suddenly, there was Dalton.

He'd just appeared, much the same way the devil himself supposedly did whenever someone called him by name.

He stepped into the stall with her and closed the door behind him.

"You . . . startled me," she accused huskily, feeling her pulse begin to race.

Although she suspected that the increased pulse rate was due more to the lecherous grin he was giving her than to anything else.

"Serves you right," he told her.

He gave her a kiss. He smelled of Dalton and of her. It was the most intoxicating fragrance she'd ever inhaled. Then he rubbed his beard-stubbled cheek against hers, sending a comforting warmth sluicing through her veins that heated her to her very core.

"If you hadn't sneaked out of my sleeping bag without so much as a good-bye," he murmured, "I wouldn't have had to resort to tracking you down in the shower."

She laughed and slid her arms around his

waist and gave him a hug, as though it were the most natural thing in the world to do.

"You were sleeping so peacefully, I didn't have the heart to wake you this morning," she said.

"This morning?" He met her gaze, held it. "You mean you stayed the night?" he asked softly.

She felt herself flush.

"I . . . yes," she said. "I hadn't meant to but I fell asleep. Fortunately, I awoke before anyone else had. It . . . it could have been a tad awkward explaining why I had spent the night in your tent."

He regarded her for a moment.

"It could have been a tad glorious too," he said. "Waking up together, I mean."

He slid his hands around her waist and pulled her closer to him until her breasts were crushed against his chest. She could feel the power of his arousal pressing hard against her lower abdomen.

She felt her heart begin to pound. She took a shaky breath.

"In fact," he went on, "the only thing better than last night would have been to roll over and find you sleeping beside me this morning."

"How so?" she murmured, feeling the heat begin to swirl around her again.

"To start with," he murmured back, "I'd

have stroked your body slowly awake. Then I'd have slid myself inside you . . . wrapped your legs around my hips . . . and made slow, languid love to you until you came, moaning my name."

His low voice sent dozens of erotic chills rocketing down her spine.

She felt her mouth go dry. The muscles in her lower abdomen began to constrict.

"I'd like to make love to you right now too," he added huskily.

She tried to suppress a shudder but couldn't.

"That . . . would be great," she said, feeling suddenly breathless. "But . . ."

She let her voice fade away.

"But what?" he murmured.

His lips nuzzled the side of her neck until she wanted to purr in feminine satisfaction, then his tongue began to rake along the same path his lips had taken, making her skin sizzle.

Liquid heat started to pool inside her again. Heaven help her, but she wanted him. Now.

"We can't. . . ." She took a deep breath. "I just think it isn't such a good idea right now."

"Oh, I think it's a great idea, sweetheart," he murmured, then tipped her chin up toward his.

His lips captured hers and began to move

across them in a kiss so sensual, it made her heart begin to flutter wildly. Then he forced his tongue inside her mouth to seek out hers. Hunger shot straight through to her core.

His hands moved to her breasts, caressing them first, then pinching each nipple between his fingers until they hardened into little peaks. She felt the backlash of the cool spray of the shower against her shoulders, but it offered little relief.

The heat was so thick around her now, she thought she could never be cooled.

"But . . . the condoms are back in the tent," she pointed out.

"So I'll be careful."

He slid his hand down her abdomen to touch her. She moaned softly and arched herself toward him.

"We both will," he added huskily.

"But . . ."

She slid her hands down to the bulge in his gym shorts. She began to massage him.

"But Ian and Brian will be awake soon," she murmured, trying to remain in control even though she knew that it was a losing battle.

How could she possibly win? Even as she tried to talk him out of making love to her, she couldn't seem to stop herself from touching him.

"They're still asleep," he told her. "It's

early still. They won't be awake for another
fifteen minutes at least."

"But—"

"Shh," he whispered, cutting her off. "You
worry too much, sweetheart. Besides . . .
right now . . . I wouldn't care if the whole
damn world found out how I felt about you."

He reached over and adjusted the spray of
water until it flowed warm and soft against her
back. Then she watched him strip off his gym
shorts and hang them on the towel hook on
the back of the door.

Seconds later, his hands were on her again.
Touching. Stroking. Caressing. And his lips
were on her mouth. Giving. Taking. Loving.
And his body was pressing hard against hers,
so hard, she started to tremble from the need
swelling up inside her.

And when she opened for him and he slid
inside her a heartbeat later, she wrapped her
arms around him and held him tight, knowing
full well that loving him again would only lead
to trouble but also knowing in her soul that
she couldn't help herself even if she tried.

She didn't seem to care about the need for
discretion or the dangers of letting herself get
close to him again.

All she cared about was his touch and his
kiss and the way he had of making her body
burn with desire, yet still make her feel so incredibly safe, as though nothing could ever

possibly harm her as long as he held her in his arms.

All she cared about was Dalton.

And she cared about him so much, it was scaring her to death.

The next five days sped past.

Mostly, Sean thought, because she'd spent nearly each waking moment with Dalton . . . as well as most of the nonwaking ones, too, when she'd been curled up beside him in the sleeping bag in his tent.

She'd never felt so comfortable with another person before in her entire life as she was with Dalton. The realization positively amazed her. When they weren't working together down at the excavation site or sharing their domestic duties at camp, they would wander off to find a quiet spot and . . . just talk.

They spent hours discussing their favorite books: Hers had been a collection of tall tales about Caribbean-based pirates, his a tie between Robert Louis Stevenson's *Treasure Island* and Mark Twain's *Tom Sawyer*. They talked about their favorite movies: They'd both admitted a fondness for the old Doris Day/Rock Hudson films, although Errol Flynn's *Captain Blood* ranked as her favorite swashbuckling film, while his was Tyrone Power's *The Black Swan.*

They discussed everything from politics and religion to their most favorite chocolate bars and their least favorite vegetables, until Sean felt as though she had known Dalton all her life.

Each little thing she discovered about him made her like him all the more, just as each little detail of her life that she shared with him seemed to make them grow closer.

When they grew tired of getting to know each other mentally, they decided to get to know each other's body better. They made love, wonderfully, glorious carnal love that lasted until neither could move. Then they slept.

Having his arms holding her tight each night became so natural, she wondered how she had ever managed to sleep before she met him—or how she would ever sleep again once he was gone. She told herself not to dwell on things she couldn't change.

That was why she tried not to think about how dependent she was becoming both on him and on the feelings that he aroused inside her.

She also tried not to think about how he hadn't said so much as a word about their pursuing a more permanent relationship since that day out at the excavation site at Area Two.

Even though she had made him promise to a no-strings-attached affair, she hadn't actually believed him when he'd agreed to her terms. In fact, for days now, she'd been anticipating that he'd make an attempt to try to get her to change her mind about their relationship. But he'd kept silent.

She guessed he was happy with the way things were between them.

Then the words of an old proverb came back to haunt her: Be careful what you wish for . . . because you just might get it.

How true, she thought.

And how unbearably sad.

After all, a no-strings-attached summer fling had been all that she'd told Dalton she wanted with him.

It was apparently all that she was going to get with him too.

Somehow knowing that she would get precisely what she'd asked for should have made her a whole helluva lot happier than she was.

On the morning of his tenth day at the expedition, Dalton settled into a white molded plastic chair beside his grandfather's hospital bed while Sean took the one next to his.

"They tell us you're trying to organize the nursing assistants into a union," Dalton said dryly. "I presume this means you're feeling better."

Samuel Gregory's tanned, weathered face split into a wide grin. His once dark brown hair was now silver, but he still wore it pulled straight back into a ponytail at the base of his neck as he had for as far back as Dalton could remember.

"Damn right I am," Samuel said jovially. "On both counts too!"

His deep voice thundered with so much vim and vigor, it was hard to believe that he'd turned eighty-one on his last birthday or that he was confined to bed for the next few weeks.

"They're overworked and underpaid," Samuel went on, his gray eyes burning with the fire of a new revolution. "Why, the staff at a convalescent home two miles away make nearly three dollars an hour more. Management keeps claiming they have no more money in the budget, so what I suggested they do was this. . . ."

Dalton glanced at Sean and grinned as his grandfather went off on one of his familiar rants. The topics had changed over the years but the message was always the same: Trust no one, question everything—especially those in authority—and always fight for the rights of those who can't fight for themselves.

"Good for you, Sammy," Sean said, once

he had finished his tale. "Shake up the status quo a bit. It sounds as though it needs it."

"Yes, but just don't overexert yourself," Dalton said, unable not to worry. "You're supposed to be convalescing, remember?"

"Nonsense," Samuel said. "I feel fine. Although that damned physical therapy feels as though they want to break my other hip."

He folded his arms against his chest. "But enough about me," he said. "Tell me about the LaRue Expedition. What news do you have?"

Sean smiled. "Well, there's really nothing much to report yet."

"Nothing much to report?" Dalton repeated with disbelief. "Last night, all you and Ian could talk about were the results of the second soil analysis from the new site."

"So you think you're onto something?" Samuel asked quickly.

Sean shifted positions in her chair.

"We set up an excavation site on Area Three a couple of days ago," she explained. "The first set of soil analyses had proven inconclusive, so Brian ran some more. He says it looks good. And the ground-penetrating radar shows there may be something down there."

"The chest?" Samuel looked as excited as a kid on Christmas morning.

"Maybe," Sean said. "More than likely, though, it's just another big rock."

Even as she tried to downplay its significance, her blue eyes were glowing with the same kind of excitement as Samuel's.

"We won't know for certain until we get down there," she added.

"What happened to all that 'oh, it's there, Dalton, I can feel it' stuff?" he teased. "Don't tell me you're losing faith in your own expedition."

"Not at all," she said, glancing at him. "I still believe the chest is somewhere near the caverns. I just don't want us to get our hopes up about Area Three. Besides," she said, grinning back at him, "you're a fine one to talk about losing faith in the expedition, since you never had much faith in it to begin with."

She turned to Samuel.

"Dalton thinks we're on a wild-goose chase, Sammy," she said. "He's never believed LaRue buried even one chest, let alone three."

"That's only because there's such blessed little historical evidence to back up the legends," Dalton reminded her. "And I think we'd have better luck finding entire flocks of wild geese than we would in uncovering La-Rue's treasure."

"Uh-huh," she said. "Care to put your money where your mouth is?"

He grinned. "What did you have in mind?"

"How about a steak dinner with all the

trimmings? I say that we will find the chest before the end of the summer."

"You're on, but make it prime rib . . . in someplace fancy."

Either way, it would give them a chance for a romantic dinner on the town. She looked good—damned good—in her shorts and T-shirts, but he'd still like to see her all dressed up in a pair of sexy high heels and an even sexier low-cut dress.

Preferably something in black.

And skintight.

He felt his body begin to respond as the image took hold in his imagination.

"It's a deal," Sean told him.

Samuel looked from Sean to Dalton and back again. Samuel arched an eyebrow, then smiled and leaned back against his pillows.

"I should have warned you, Sean," Samuel said.

"Dalton's always been the sensible type. He got it from his father, although I'm sure it was a genetic trait that I never passed on."

Dalton laughed.

"Well, sometimes being sensible is a good thing," Sean said.

"Yes, and sometimes so is going with what you feel in your heart," Samuel said. "It's all about balance. Go too far in either direction, and you'll end up hurting yourself in the long run.

"Besides," he went on. "Whether the chest is there or not isn't the important thing. Not for me, anyway. I was always interested in the adventure. And what a grand adventure it was!"

His eyes took on a faraway look. "I only spent two weeks with the expedition, but those two weeks made me feel decades younger. And look what it's done for Dalton. Why, he's a new man! He's relaxed, happy. I bet that you're having the time of your life out at the camp, aren't you, my boy?"

Dalton smiled. "That I am," he said. "Even if I don't quite believe we'll ever find LaRue's treasure, it's a little hard not to get caught up in all the excitement of the expedition."

Or to get caught up in Sean herself.

He felt he was so attuned to her, he could probably finish her sentences for her.

Just as he sometimes felt that he could feel each beat of her heart when they made love . . . along with each sigh of feminine pleasure when he stroked her in the right spot.

He reached for her hand, wrapped his fingers around her palm, and gave it a light squeeze.

"You needed a little excitement in your life," Samuel said. "You've spent far too much time locked away at the university. Academia is all well and good, but it feeds the mind and starves the soul."

Dalton smiled. His grandfather was right. There were things missing in his life.

Lately, Dalton had been thinking that he needed to make a lot of changes, most of which involved making Sean a permanent addition to his life. Even without her objections to a long-term relationship, he knew it would be hard to try to maintain one as long as he was living in Georgia and she in Florida, with her work taking her away for months at a time.

"I've been considering taking a sabbatical," he said. "Maybe start work on a novel that I've been thinking about doing."

Sean looked at him quizzically for a moment, but didn't say anything.

"Good idea," Samuel said. "You're a fine teacher, but the university has become your life over the past few years. That's not healthy. A job shouldn't have that much power over anyone, especially when there is a whole world out there to be explored."

Samuel turned to Sean.

"The same advice holds true for you, my dear," he said. "I know how long you've searched for LaRue's treasure, and I know how hard you've worked at making Setarip a success. But you're a warm, giving woman. As exciting as the adventure of seeking out lost treasures may be, it's nothing compared to the adventure of love."

Sean started to flush and slipped her hand out of Dalton's.

"Now you're being silly, Sammy," she said. "I'm happy with my life."

"Nonsense," Samuel said. "You're as bad as Dalton, although to the other extreme. That's why you two make such a great couple."

"But we're not a couple," Sean said quickly. "Dalton and I are just . . ."

Her voice faded away as though she didn't know how to define their relationship. Dalton felt something tighten inside him.

He glanced at Sean. He tried to capture her gaze but couldn't.

"Sean and I are just friends, Samuel," Dalton said quietly.

"Friends?" Samuel repeated softly, his voice losing some of its earlier vigor. "That's really too bad, because it's plain to see that you both want more."

Sean sighed. "Sammy . . ."

Samuel's gaze shot toward her. "Don't 'Sammy' me, girl," he said, cutting her off. "You and Dalton belong together, and you know it."

Then Samuel smiled. "Once the expedition is over, why don't you two run off somewhere together? Settle down. Make a passel of babies. Have a *real* adventure for a change."

The color seemed to drain from Sean's face.

"Babies?" She twisted uncomfortably in her chair. *"Babies?"*

Then the door swung open and a heavyset nurse in her late fifties came into the room carrying a small plastic tray with paper cups of medication.

"Time for your pills, sugar," she drawled. "And don't you give me none of your backtalk about it this time, neither."

Samuel nodded and motioned for the woman to come toward him.

"Life's too short, Sean," he said, continuing the thread of their conversation. "When a chance for happiness comes along, you need to embrace it with every ounce of strength you have, regardless of the risk."

He reached for the medication cup. He tossed the pills into his mouth, swallowed, then chased them down with a glass of water handed to him by the nurse.

"And if you're not willing to take a risk on your own happiness," Samuel went on, "what the hell *are* you willing to take a risk on?"

Samuel met Sean's gaze, held it a moment, then glanced at Dalton and did the same.

"Well?" Samuel demanded.

Dalton didn't answer. Neither did Sean.

Samuel shook his head. "For both your sakes, I hope you figure it out soon."

Dalton sighed.

So did he.

EIGHT

Sean didn't say much during the short walk from Sammy's room down the bustling corridor of the extended-care nursing facility and out the rear exit to the tree-shaded parking lot.

She shot him several glances when she thought he wasn't looking. She couldn't help it, just as she couldn't help but wonder what his reaction had been to his grandfather's piece of unsolicited advice . . . especially the part concerning their need to pursue a shared life, complete with parenthood.

Dalton hadn't said so much as a single, solitary word in Sammy's room about it, and he didn't appear ready to comment about it now.

Or anytime soon.

Still, Dalton's hands were shoved into the pockets of his khaki shorts and his forehead was wrinkled in serious thought, so she knew that he was ruminating over something or the other.

She'd have given almost everything she owned to know what those thoughts were.

Once they'd settled into his cream-colored Toyota Camry, Dalton started the ignition, clicked on the air-conditioning, then slipped a Collin Raye cassette into the tape deck. He turned up the volume as he pulled out onto the main road.

They spoke little during the drive back to Sammy's converted farmhouse. When they did speak, it was mostly meaningless chitchat about the traffic—it was unexpectedly heavy on Gulf Breeze Highway for that time of day. And the weather—dark thunderclouds were slowly rolling in from the coast, which meant a summer storm was headed their way.

Sean told herself that she should be glad that Dalton didn't want to talk. She had too much on her mind, too many emotions of her own to sort through, to have a serious conversation.

Still, a part of her wished that he would say something so that she could talk about the feelings tumbling through her.

A part of her even wished that she were brave enough to initiate the conversation herself.

But she wasn't.

So she didn't.

Thirty minutes later, Dalton pulled the Toyota inside the two-car garage and parked next to Sammy's red Ford Bronco.

Dalton switched off the ignition and slowly turned toward her.

"I've got to make a quick phone call to my parents," he said, his voice more somber than usual. "Let them know how Samuel's doing."

She met his gaze, feeling a little confused. "But I thought that Sammy wasn't on speaking terms with your parents."

"They aren't," he said. "He and my father haven't said so much as a civil word to each other in years. But Dad still loves Samuel, just as I know that Samuel still loves my dad. I promised to keep my parents updated. It'll only take a couple of minutes."

She nodded. "Okay."

She opened the car door and swung her feet out to the concrete.

"I'll meet you back in the laundry room," he said.

It had been her week for laundry detail, so they'd done a couple loads of dirty clothes before leaving for the convalescent home.

"Take your time," she told him.

She shut the car door and headed right, toward the laundry room, which was adjacent to the garage.

The dryer had already clicked off, but the

clothes inside it were still warm. She started to shake them out, one at a time, and fold them into neat stacks in the large wicker laundry basket, letting her thoughts wander as she worked.

A lot of what Sammy had said had made sense. A lot she had disagreed with, though. As for his comment about her settling down with Dalton and having babies . . . well, that had come completely out of the blue.

And just how many babies did it take to compose a passel? Sean wondered, shaking her head in disbelief. Two? Three?

A dozen?

As ridiculous as the suggestion had been, however, she had to admit that there were times when she'd thought about starting a family of her own.

There were times when she thought about it so much that the sight of a mother and her newborn child could cut her straight to the bone.

Sean wanted that sense of belonging that only having children could bring, although she'd always tried to keep those feelings locked away inside her. Why should she let herself ache for something that she knew she could never have?

Still . . .

The ache never quite went away.

It probably never would.

Realizing that didn't change the fact that she wasn't sure if she could let herself trust any man enough to make him a permanent part of her life.

It also didn't change the fact that she wasn't at all sure if she would make a good mother.

After all, genetics probably accounted for a large part of the maternal instinct, and there were few sterling examples of motherhood perched on the branches of her family tree.

As for Dalton being a father . . . well, that was different. She somehow knew that he'd make a good one. He'd likely be the same kind of father as he was a man. Good. Strong. Loving.

He'd be the kind of dad who would be there for Little League practices, as well as the Big Game. He'd be the kind who'd be there to help with homework and to chase the bogeyman from the closet. He'd be there for birthdays and holidays and family suppers . . . and just plain growing up.

Most of all, he would be the kind of dad who wouldn't decide the responsibility of having a family was simply too great to bear and opt for an easy out, the way her own father had done.

Sean took a slow, deep breath.

Damn, she thought, feeling the tears of a lifetime begin to well up inside her.

This wasn't good, she decided.

No, it wasn't good at all.

When Dalton walked into the laundry room about fifteen minutes later, Sean had just placed the last of the towels into the wicker basket.

"Sorry I took so long," he told her. "I couldn't seem to get my mom off the phone."

She glanced up. There was a shadow of sadness haunting her blue eyes. For a moment he wondered if she'd been crying.

The possibility that she had suddenly sent an icy chill thundering through him that settled around the vicinity of his heart.

"No problem," she said.

Then she gave him a smile and the shadows nearly disappeared.

"How are your parents?" she asked.

"Fine," he said, walking toward her.

He kept his gaze locked on her face.

"I, ah, tried to get them to fly down and visit Samuel," he went on. "Dad said no—in some rather strong language—but Mom said she'd talk to him about it. Samuel would react much the same way to Dad's coming to visit, I imagine."

"What happened between them?" She frowned and dropped the lid into place on the basket. "Your father and Samuel, I mean."

He shrugged. "It was a presidential election . . . about ten years ago. I don't remember the specific details. Basically, a difference of opinion led to harsh words and they haven't spoken since."

"Sounds pretty damned silly to me," she said.

It was.

"I agree," he told her. "And it's high time this feud of theirs was ended too."

"Good. Family is important."

It may have been his imagination, but he could have sworn that her voice sounded a tad huskier than normal.

"You should tell Sammy that I said so," she added sternly.

"I will."

A few seconds passed.

A tendril of her hair had escaped from its French braid. He traced a fingertip along the silky strand.

"Hey," he said softly.

She looked up. Their gazes locked.

"Are you okay?" he asked.

She flushed. "I'm fine. Why do you ask?"

Maybe it was something in her eyes . . . or something in her soul . . . or maybe something in his that told him she was still in pain from a long-ago hurt.

"I was just wondering if you were upset by what Samuel said this afternoon," he murmured. "Because I swear to you, Sean, I don't know where he came up with that idea about our getting married."

She gave him a smile. "He didn't say we should get *married*, Dalton," she corrected. "He said we should make babies. Lots of them, in fact."

He grinned. "Samuel always has been blunt in expressing his opinions."

"I know," she said. "And it's okay. He . . . he even made a few valid points."

"Oh?"

She nodded. "Like the part where he said we need to take a chance on ourselves," she said. "I think he's right. I took a chance on myself when I opened Setarip, and I've never regretted it. Speaking of which . . ."

She leaned down and picked up the basket of folded laundry.

"Are you ready to head back to camp?" she asked.

His hands slid over hers, stopping her.

"What's the hurry?" he asked huskily.

She met his gaze again. Her cheeks began to flush.

"Well, I've already lost most of the day as it is," she said. "I can't justify wasting any more time. I need to get back to work."

He glided his hands up her arms to her shoulders, skimming over the lightly tanned skin with a barely perceptible touch, yet he still felt the shivers shimmering through her.

He cupped her chin in his hands and tilted her head back to meet her gaze.

"If LaRue's chest has survived this long out there in the marsh, it ought to survive another hour, sweetheart," he said.

He brushed the pads of his thumbs along her jawline, still amazed at the softness of her skin.

He was also amazed that he could want her with such an all-consuming hunger, even after having spent the past week making love to her nearly every chance he'd gotten.

Liquid heat began to flow through his veins. His mouth went dry.

"You know," he murmured, "now that I think about it, that chest ought to survive another two hours easily. Maybe even three."

She laughed, low and husky.

The sound still got to him as much as it had the first time he'd heard it.

He suspected it probably always would.

Just as Sean herself would probably always get to him, no matter how much time might pass.

He smiled. He didn't think that he would have had it any other way.

Wanting her, having her want him back . . . loving her, having her love him back . . . it seemed the most natural thing in the world to him.

"Hmm. Feeling a little amorous today, are we?" she teased.

She dropped the laundry basket to the floor and ran her hands up his abdomen and chest to rest on his shoulders. The warm pressure of her palms scorched through the lightweight cotton of his shirt, burning his skin.

Branding his soul.

"Hmm," he murmured back. "Could be."

He kissed the light dusting of copper-colored freckles across the bridge of her nose. He'd counted them once when she had been sleeping in his arms. She had precisely twenty-three.

So he gave her precisely twenty-three tiny kisses, one for each freckle.

He started at her forehead, then moved quickly down to her eyes and the tip of her nose, then across her cheeks and down to her chin, until he had covered nearly every inch of her face with feather-soft kisses.

"Why don't you tell me what you think I'm feeling," he suggested.

Then he pushed the laundry basket to one side with the tip of his sneaker and pulled her closer until her slender body was intimately aligned with his . . . then closer still until his arousal pressed hard and strong against her lower abdomen.

He began to ache for her, but it was an ache and a need for more than just a physical release.

He ached to know that she loved him, the same way that he loved her.

Without hesitation.

Without question.

"I . . . oh, I think that you probably are feeling a tad frisky," she said huskily. "But it's okay. You see, I like it when you're feeling amorous. I like it a lot."

He grinned. He grazed the curve of one delicate earlobe with his tongue, taking delight in the way she murmured her pleasure at his touch, then worked his way down her neck to the hollow of her throat.

He could feel the mad flutter of her pulse beating rapidly against his lips.

It made his own pulse race faster.

"So do I, sweetheart," he told her. His voice was raw with hunger. "So do I."

He reached for her mouth and moved his lips over hers in a kiss so deliberately soft and slow and sensual, it was designed to make her sigh and melt against him.

She wound her arms around his back and clung to him, kissing him with such wild abandon and hunger and need, it threatened to bring him to his knees.

He groaned and deepened the kiss, wanting to turn her previous sigh into a moan. He slid his tongue into her mouth to seek out hers, sucking, massaging, stroking, taking joy in her unbridled response. He could kiss her forever.

He almost did.

Sometime later, he pulled back slightly to meet her gaze again, needing to see hunger and need burning in her eyes instead of the pain he'd seen there earlier.

He got his wish. Her gaze practically sizzled with desire.

He gave her a grin. "Have I mentioned that there's a bed waiting for us upstairs in my old room? Wrought-iron posters? Soft, comfy mattress?"

"No," she said. "You didn't . . . and that sounds wonderful."

She began to massage his shoulders, pressing her fingertips into his tight muscles. Rather than relaxing him, the tender strokes only made his body grow harder.

"A bed would be a welcome change after all those sleeping bags," she said.

"My thoughts exactly," he murmured.

Then he grasped the sides of her T-shirt and pulled it up so he could plant a kiss in the middle of her cleavage. The floral scent of her perfume swirled around him, fogging his brain until he couldn't think, until he could only feel.

His body began to ache with need. His arousal strained against his khaki shorts.

He raked his tongue along the curves of her full breasts, loving their smoothness and their softness, loving the way her skin tasted. But it wasn't enough, not nearly enough.

He wanted to taste *her*.

All of her.

He began to wet a nipple through the lacy fabric of her bra until it grew hard and pebbled against his tongue, then he switched to the other one and did the same. She murmured his name as though it were a prayer and ran her fingers through his hair.

Her voice, more than her touch, sent an electric thrill vibrating through him that made the need within him become more urgent.

He stripped off her shirt and dropped it on top of the laundry basket, then reached around her back to unclasp her bra. Her breasts fell heavy and soft into his open palms. He lowered his head and drew a nipple into his mouth, gently suckling her.

He strummed his hand down her abdomen to grasp the metal snap of her cutoff jeans. He popped open the snap, then slowly unzipped her shorts.

"I . . . Dalton?"

"What, baby?"

He slid his hand inside her shorts and felt the damp heat of her feminine core burning through her cotton panties. He slipped his fingers past the lacy edge of her panties and started to stroke her. A low moan escaped her throat, and she moved her hips against his hand.

She was ready, he thought.

So was he.

"You . . . you drive me crazy when you touch me like that," she murmured huskily.

"Good," he said. "I like you crazy . . . crazy with need . . . crazy with hunger."

He slowly withdrew his hand and met her gaze.

"I want to make you crazier still," he said. "I want to make you so crazy that you come against my tongue."

"I . . ." She shuddered.

He wrapped his hands around her waist and lifted her up to sit on top of the still-warm dryer. Then he began to tug her shorts and panties down her hips. She raised herself up and he grasped the clothes and pulled them down her long, tanned legs until they rested on the tops of her work boots. She kicked her feet free, and the shorts and panties landed on the floor.

She reached for her shoelaces. He stopped her.

"Later," he whispered, opening her legs and moving in between them. "I want to taste you, sweetheart. I can't wait."

He brushed his lips against the soft skin of her inner thighs, feeling the fever burning inside her for him as acutely as he did his own desire for her. He slowly kissed his way up to her mound of soft red curls. The musky scent of her washed over him, making his body tighten all the harder.

Then he slid his tongue over her sex, feeling her tense, loving the way that she gasped in sheer feminine delight and clutched at his hair. He raked his tongue over her again. Then again. Wetting her each time. Teasing her too. And tasting her.

Loving her.

"What . . . what happened to going upstairs to use your old bedroom?" she asked breathlessly.

"Nothing," he said.

He slid his fingers inside her and started to stroke her. He felt her body begin to spasm and slowed the rhythm of his touching.

He raised his head and watched her face. Her skin was flushed, her eyes glittered with unchecked passion.

"Just a slight delay in plans, that's all," he said huskily, and lowered his head again.

He was enjoying the sweet, sweet torment he was bringing to Sean far too much for him to be able to stop.

"Just . . . checking," she whispered, and shuddered against his hand again.

Then he licked his tongue over the sensitized nub of her desire and intensified his efforts to pleasure her with his hands and with his tongue until she moaned his name and arched her hips toward his mouth . . . and spiraled out of control.

Sean had almost dozed off to sleep in Dalton's arms when she heard the front door open and slam hard against the living-room wall.

She sat bolt upright in bed, clutching the gray-and-white-striped bedspread to her chest.

Apprehension shot through her. Her heart began to pound.

"Dalton?"

"I heard it," he told her softly.

He gave her a kiss on her cheek, which immediately calmed her. Then he pushed off the covers and climbed out of bed. He reached for his briefs and tugged them on, then grabbed his shorts. He was out the door in less than a heartbeat.

Sean slowly slid out of bed and reached for her clothes. She'd tossed them into a crumpled heap on the carpeted floor after their mad dash upstairs from the laundry room.

Seconds later, she heard movement from the living room, Dalton's voice, then the unmistakable sound of a rebel yell rang out, loud enough to take the curl right out of her hair.

"Ian," she whispered.

She'd recognize his yell anywhere.

Seconds later, she heard Dalton give a whoop of excitement of his own.

By the time Sean reached the top of the stairs, Ian and Dalton were already patting each other on the back in typical male fashion. They also had wide, irrepressible grins on their faces.

"What happened?" she asked.

Even as she asked the question she felt she knew the answer.

After all, there was only one reason that Ian ever gave his famous rebel yell.

Ian's grin grew wider. "We hit paydirt."

"What?" she asked hoarsely.

She tucked her T-shirt into her shorts, then took the stairs two at a time in her bare feet.

"Brian and I kept going this morning after you guys left," Ian went on. "I hit something when I reached seven feet. I used the drill to do an exploratory and . . . we'd struck wood."

He still carried the dirt-and-mud-coated drill in his hand. Shards of wood—and old wood at that—clung to the bit . . . along with a long strand of what appeared to be a gleaming yellow chain.

"And then we struck gold," he added.

Her heart simply stopped.

"Gold?" she whispered.

Her mouth went dry.

Ian nodded. "It was probably from some kind of filigreed necklace. Definitely museum quality, whatever it had been. If the rest of LaRue's cache are the same caliber, the haul can easily net us somewhere in the low seven digits."

"Oh my God," she whispered.

Then Ian wrapped his arms around her and gave her a giant bear hug that nearly squeezed the life right out of her. She didn't even mind the drill pressing painfully into the center of her back.

"We did it, sis," he whispered in her ear. "Just like you always said we would."

After he released her, Ian turned to Dalton. "Where's the phone? I need to call the office, get a crew out here to start the recovery operations. And Brian wants a couple of pizzas delivered. You like pepperoni?"

"Phone's in the kitchen," Dalton said, pointing out the direction. "I love pepperoni."

Ian let go with another rebel yell that shook the rafters, then headed off to the kitchen at a fast trot to make the calls.

Sean couldn't move, however.

She felt as though her feet were nailed to the floorboards.

They'd done it, she thought, trying to absorb the information. They'd actually found one of LaRue's three chests.

Dalton glanced at her.

Their gazes met, held.

"Congratulations," he told her softly. "Guess this means I owe you a prime-rib dinner."

"Yeah," she said. "I guess you do."

Then just as suddenly as the exhilaration of victory had swept over her, it started to dissipate, leaving her with a slightly queasy feeling in the pit of her stomach.

When he looked at her, she realized that while she may have won the battle, she'd probably lost the war.

After all, they'd located the chest. That meant the expedition was officially over, except for the recovery efforts.

It also meant that very soon now, Dalton would be leaving for his home and his life back in Georgia.

As would she to her own in Florida.

And there was damned little she could do to stop it from happening.

NINE

Dalton was amazed by the speed with which Setarip swung into action following Ian's telephone call.

A six-man crew and several large pieces of equipment arrived by eight o'clock the next morning. By noon, the hydraulic lifts needed to remove the chest from the water-soaked ground had been set up next to the site, along with a pair of high-tech water pumps in case the excavation pit flooded from underground streams.

Flooding was a distinct possibility, Ian had explained, citing Oak Island as a good example of the need to proceed with caution. The Nova Scotian site was famous for its cache of pirate treasure supposedly buried deep in a water-filled pit, which had defied recovery efforts for nearly two hundred years. While it was doubtful that Jackson LaRue had installed booby traps in the marsh, as Captain Kidd is credited with doing at Oak Island, there was always a natural risk of danger from water in a marsh.

Mother Nature was also proving contrary. Weather forecasts still predicted a major storm front headed their way, which meant they'd have to move quickly before rain filled the pit and caused the chest to sink even farther into the ground.

Knowing that he would likely only get in the way if he tried to help, Dalton sat back and watched the experts go to work.

Mostly, though, he watched Sean.

She seemed to be in her element now. She ran the recovery effort with skill and precision, barking commands with the kind of confidence that one of her beloved pirates might have envied, and it was clear that her crew respected her, too.

Seeing her like this—seeing her strong and capable and glowing with excitement—made Dalton love her all the more. He decided that he was proud of her too. He was proud of the way that she'd accomplished the seemingly impossible, proud of the way that she'd refused to give up regardless of how many times that he—and he was sure countless others—had told her that finding the LaRue treasure simply could not be done.

He was proud of the way that she'd stubbornly clung to a childhood dream until she'd made it become a reality.

He'd hoped to have a chance to tell her all of those things himself, but so far he hadn't.

Sean was too busy.

A dull ache began to grow in his chest as he watched her work.

She'd been so *busy* that she hadn't spent the previous night with him. Instead, she'd given him an excuse about needing to get some rest before the recovery began and had returned to her tent.

She'd been so *busy* that she had declined his suggestion that they go for a walk through the marsh that morning to talk because the crew would be arriving soon and she needed to prepare.

In short, she'd been so damned *busy* that she hadn't given him so much as a minute of her attention, undivided or otherwise, since Ian's announcement of the chest's discovery.

And it scared Dalton.

It scared him straight through to his core, because he couldn't help but remember their agreement that the end of their love affair would be marked by one of two events.

The end of summer. Or the discovery of the chest.

He felt that dull ache inside him become

sharper, more acute. It was like the twist of
the blade of a knife through his heart.

It wasn't fair, dammit, he thought. He
loved her.

And whether Sean wanted to admit it or
not, he knew that she loved him too.

The problem, unfortunately, was how to
convince her of that. Assuming, of course, that
he still would have the chance.

Dalton frowned.

"Son-of-a-bitch!"

Sean flinched as Ian's voice rose up from
the bottom of the excavation pit.

The curse was quickly followed by a
"Watch it!" from Rick Morales, one of the
other crew members working with Ian. Then
came the rattle of chains and a dull thud as
those same chains hit against the side of the
chest.

One of the heavy metal cables suspended
from the hydraulic lift started to shake. Sean
slipped on her work gloves, then reached out
and grabbed the cable, pulling it steady. She
peered into the pit.

"Everything okay?"

Rick was bent over the chest, attaching the
chains. He waved a hand in the air as if to say
everything was fine but didn't turn around.

She frowned. "Ian?"

Ian looked up at her. Mud streaked his face and his nose was beginning to peel from the sunburn. He also looked tired. No wonder, since he and Rick had been crawling around in what was basically a giant mud hole for the past hour, trying to dig out the chest enough so they could attach the chains in order for the hydraulic lift to pull the chest from the pit.

But a wide grin still split across Ian's face. In fact, she'd never seen him look happier than he did right at that moment.

"Everything's fine," he told her. "I just pinched my finger with one of the clamps."

"Which he then tried to hit me with when he flung the chain," Rick muttered good-naturedly.

Ian laughed.

She shook her head at both of them. "Be careful," she said, smiling.

Lightning flashed in the distance, followed by the ominous roll of thunder.

She glanced up at the sky. The summer storm that had been threatening for the past couple of days looked as though it was finally ready to strike.

It promised to be a real doozy.

The air was already thick and muggy from the impending rain.

"Just hurry," she told them. "I either want

the chest out of there before the storm hits or the site closed down. You've got five minutes."

"We can do it," Ian promised her. "Don't worry."

She stepped back from the edge of the pit. She wasn't so sure if Ian could deliver. The storm was rolling in fast. She told herself that she should probably tell him to abandon the attempt for the day and have the crew secure the site against the elements before the storm hit, but she didn't.

She simply couldn't.

She understood only too well Ian's determination to bring the chest out now without waiting another hour, let alone another day.

After all, they'd been planning and preparing for this moment for most of their lives. To have finally come this close to finding LaRue's treasure . . . well, she knew that Ian wasn't about to let a little thing like a thunderstorm stop him.

She doubted if he'd have even stopped if a hurricane were about to blow through.

Sean pulled off the gloves and stuck them under the edge of her utility belt. All she could do now was wait, just as most of the crew had been doing for the past hour while Ian and Rick tried to secure the chains.

She scanned the excavation site. Two of the crew members had video cameras, which they were using to record the recovery.

They'd used them so frequently on past treasure hunts, she hardly even noticed them now.
A representative from the state department of
revenue was there also to document the find
for tax purposes.

Her gaze sought out Dalton, just as she'd
found it doing for most of the day.

The last time she'd seen him, he had been
leaning against a pine tree chatting with one
of the team members. Now he was sitting on
the flatbed of the transport truck with Brian.
The truck's heavy canvas covering was pulled
back against its cab, ready to accommodate
the placement of the chest.

For hours she'd told herself to stop watching Dalton. She'd told herself to keep her attention focused on the job.

It was damned hard to do either, though.

She hadn't been able to take her gaze off
him since the moment they'd first met.

It was funny, really. Here she was, teeter-
ing on the brink of what should have been one
of the most momentous occasions of her
life . . . yet all she could think about was
Dalton.

All she wanted to think about was how his
smile and his voice and the gentle stroke of his
hand against her face seemed to make her feel
more cherished and more safe than she had
ever felt in her entire life.

All she wanted to think about was how

much she was going to miss him once he left—because she was missing him so much already, it was nearly killing her.

"Got it!" Rick called out.

Sean took a deep breath. Focus, she told herself.

Now.

She moved toward the edge of the pit again.

"Ready?" she called down.

"Ready," Ian replied. "Go for it, sis. Go!"

The two men started to scramble up the rope ladder secured over the side of the pit.

Sean nodded at Johnny Witherspoon, the balding, fiftyish operator of the crane.

"Let's do it," she said.

He nodded back and the hydraulic lift began to whir. The machinery seemed to pause a moment, then the slack in the cables was picked up and they began to rewind, slowly pulling the chest up from the pit.

A cheer rang out from the rest of the crew, who started to move toward the pit and watch. It was easy to spot the accountant from the revenue office. Mike Lederman, a dark-haired man in his late thirties, was the only one at the site wearing a suit. He began walking toward the crane, wiping off his perspiration-dampened forehead with a once-white handkerchief, which he then tucked back inside his interior jacket pocket.

Seeing the suit reminded her of Dalton and how ridiculous he'd looked that first day in his tweed jacket and tie . . . and how incredibly handsome too.

Her gaze moved to find him once more. He was no longer in the truck because Brian was driving it around the excavation site to meet up with the crane.

It took her only a second to find Dalton. She had a built-in radar where he was concerned. He was on his way to the pit, his hands shoved into the pockets of his dark-colored shorts.

He caught her gaze and gave her a grin.

It was one of his vintage pirate ones.

She felt its heat down to the soles of her feet.

She started to smile back, then Ian said something and she turned toward the crane.

The chest was halfway to the surface. Ian had stripped off his dirty T-shirt and was wiping his face.

"What?" she asked him.

"I said . . . are we opening her here or are we waiting until we're back at the warehouse?"

The chest and its contents would have to be inventoried and their market value assessed, a process that could very well take weeks, which was the primary reason Lederman was there.

"Let's do it here," she said. "Otherwise the crew will mutiny."

Ian gave her a grin. "You'd better believe it. Hell, I'd lead the revolt."

She reached for the gloves and pulled them back on, then moved toward the edge of the pit.

Thunder pealed again. Closer this time.

"A little further," she called out to Johnny, the crane operator. She reached behind her and waved her arm, motioning for additional pull. "Just a little more."

She could see the chest now. It was oak, with once-shiny metal handles on its side, and a large antiquated lock securing the clasp. The metal had turned a mottled shade of green and clumps of mud and earth still coated the sides of the chest.

She motioned for the crane operator to stop, and he did. She reached out for the cables. Ian and Rick moved into position beside her to help.

Working as a unit, they guided the chest toward them, then waited for Brian to back the truck closer. Once the truck was in position, they tugged the cables and walked toward the flatbed, pulling the chest with them.

Sean's shoulder muscles began to ache. Perspiration ran down her back until her shirt felt as though it were plastered to her skin.

They maneuvered the chest above the center of the flatbed, careful to avoid the metal frame used by the canvas covering.

"Let her down," Sean called over her shoulder to the crane operator.

He complied, and the chest slowly dropped into place on the back of the truck with a thump. The truck swayed a bit from the impact of the weight.

Sean felt her heart begin to pound. Whatever it was that the chest contained, it was heavy. Then she, Ian, and Rick scrambled onto the back of the truck and started to remove the chains.

"Well," Ian said, once they were done. "Aren't you going to open it?"

She glanced back at Mike Lederman. He was grinning as much as her brother.

"Go ahead," Lederman told her.

Sean glanced at Ian.

"You found it, Mudbug," she said. "You should be the one to open it."

He shook his head. "Naw, it's your baby. Always has been."

Rick jumped down off the truck to stand next to Lederman and Brian.

Ian handed her a pair of metal cutters, but she didn't have the heart to cut off the lock. Besides, the metal was so rusted, she suspected it no longer worked. She put down the shears and shook the lock until it broke apart into her hands. She laid the pieces of the lock on the flatbed next to the chest.

Sean smoothed her gloved hands over the mud-encrusted wood of the chest. She wasn't sure what she would find inside. It could be filled with gold doubloons or it could turn out to be little more than an elaborate ruse by La-Rue to impress his teenage mistress, Elizabeth Martene.

But Sean's instincts told her the chest would contain one third of LaRue's treasure, which, by all accounts, had been worth a small fortune.

Ian's discovery of the filigreed gold chain after he'd drilled into the top of the chest seemed to confirm her theories.

"Geez," Ian said. "What are you waiting for?"

Sean glanced over her shoulder again, looking for Dalton this time. She found him standing off to one side with his arms folded against his chest, watching her as intensely as she had watched him earlier.

"Dalton?" Her voice nearly cracked.

He uncrossed his arms and moved through the cluster of team members to reach the back of the truck.

"You should be here," she said.

"Samuel should be here," he corrected. "He's the one who believed in you. I was the skeptic, remember?"

"You're a part of this, Dalton," she told him. "As much a part as any of us have been. Besides, I . . . I want you here."

He smiled, climbed into the truck, and knelt down beside her next to the trunk.

"Open it, Sean," he said softly.

"Yeah, sis," Ian grumbled. "Open the damn thing already."

Lightning flashed again. Thunder quickly followed.

Sean swallowed. They were right. She shouldn't put it off any longer.

She turned back, took a deep breath, and tugged on the lid. It didn't budge. She applied more pressure and the lid popped open.

Dozens of gold doubloons tumbled from the chest to clatter against the metal bottom of the flatbed until they nearly covered her feet.

She gasped and raised the lid higher. The chest was filled to overflowing with pirate booty. More than she had ever seen gathered together in one spot: Ornately decorated goblets encrusted with precious gems, leather pouches filled with gold and silver coins, a pair of sturdy silver candlesticks. Emerald brooches. Rubies too.

All this and more.

Then the rain came. It started as a light sprinkle but quickly built to a steady downpour as the thunder rolled, heavier than before.

Ian let out another rebel yell and jumped off the truck to do a victory dance in the rain. The rest of the team members, including Lederman, joined in until pandemonium reigned supreme at the excavation site.

Sean, however, just lifted a handful of rain-splattered doubloons and turned to look at Dalton in amazement.

He stared back at her, a peculiar, undecipherable expression on his face.

"Happy?" he asked softly, so softly she almost didn't hear him.

She nodded.

"Good," he told her.

Then he gave her a kiss on her cheek that seemed unbearably sad somehow.

"I'm glad you finally got what you wanted," he murmured, and climbed off the truck.

All the happiness she felt suddenly vanished.

She knew then that there was something she'd wanted far longer than finding LaRue's chest . . . and she was watching it walk away from her.

Maybe for good.

Back at camp forty-five minutes later, Dalton parted the heavy canvas siding of the main tent and ducked inside out of the rain.

It had been pouring nearly nonstop since the storm hit, and his clothes were soaked through to his skin. He felt chilled, too, but it wasn't from the rain.

No, the chill he felt was the kind that came from a coldness of the heart.

And the only thing that could possibly warm him was a tall, leggy redhead who was too afraid to let herself fall in love.

His gaze moved toward Sean.

She stood quietly in a corner dismantling some of the high-tech computer equipment. She looked just as cold and wet as he felt . . . and a lot less happy than he would have expected a woman to look after having found a fortune in pirate treasure, which gave him hope.

He ran a hand through his hair, shook some of the water loose, and started toward her.

They were the only two still left at camp. Ian, Brian, and Mike Lederman from the revenue department had accompanied the transport truck and its cargo back to the rented warehouse in downtown Pensacola. The rest of the crew had followed in separate vehicles. Despite the storm, they were planning a big celebration in town, complete with loud music and lots of beer. After the day they'd had, Dalton couldn't say he blamed them.

He hadn't gone, though, because he hadn't felt much in the partying mood.

Neither, apparently, had Sean.

"I'm surprised you're not at the warehouse with the chest," he told her. "Standing guard over the treasure with that shotgun of yours."

He had hoped to get a smile from her. He had needed to get a smile from her.

She didn't even look up.

"We've got a security team in place at the warehouse," she said quietly.

She wrapped a power cord around a computer keyboard and placed it into a heavy cardboard box containing one of the printers.

"Anyway, there's nothing much to be done with the chest right now," she went on. "We'll need to do an inventory of its contents and then assess their value, but that can take several weeks. Maybe longer."

"I . . . see," he said.

He regarded her for a moment.

"So why aren't you out celebrating with the crew?" he asked.

She shrugged. "We've got a thunderstorm and several thousands of dollars' worth of research equipment sitting unprotected in the tent. Somebody needed to stay and keep watch. I volunteered."

On its surface, her answer sounded perfectly plausible. After all, the expedition did have expensive computer equipment sitting in the tent, and it was raining heavily.

But the tent in question had been designed to withstand far rougher weather than this.

If there had been any actual danger to the equipment from the storm, the crew would have never left camp to celebrate.

She slid a couple of pieces of Styrofoam over the sides of a monitor and set it in another box.

"I figured I might as well get an early start on packing," she added. "It'll take us a couple of days to get everything boxed and out of here."

A couple of days, he thought. That's how much longer he had with her.

He swallowed hard.

There were so many things he wanted to say. So many things he needed to hear her say to him in return. The problem was he didn't know where to start . . . or even if he should.

He had no choice but to try. He had no more time to wait for her to come to her senses.

"You did good out there, Sean," he said softly. "Real good. I admit I never thought you could pull it off . . . finding the treasure, I mean . . . but you did. I'm proud of you."

She looked up and met his gaze. "Thanks," she said. "That means a lot."

She lifted the box with the monitor and set it on the ground.

He regarded her for a moment. "Sean . . . sweetheart . . ."

He took a deep breath and tried again. "We need to talk."

She looked up and took a deep breath of her own.

"Yeah," she said. "I guess we do."

He nodded. "About what happens next."

She folded her arms against her chest.

"Well . . ." She glanced down at her feet. "Setarip will have the excavation pit filled in. We'll try to return the property to its pre-expedition condition, if possible, just like we promised Sammy. As for the treasure . . . Sammy's share is twenty-five percent, which he said he wanted to donate to charity. You're more than welcome to sit through the accounting session, or have a representative do so."

He scowled at her. "I don't care about the division of the treasure, and I don't give a damn when you decide to fill in the pit."

"Oh?" Her gaze locked with his.

"No," he said firmly. "What I want to talk about is us."

A few seconds passed.

It grew so quiet that the only sound in the

tent was the steady pelting of the rain against the heavy canvas sheeting.

"About what . . . happens . . . now, Sean. About where we go from here."

"You know the answer to that as well as I do," she said huskily.

"I know what you told me before," he said. "I just need to know if that's still true."

"Why wouldn't it be?"

Because it can't be, he thought. *Because I can't walk away from this and try to pretend that none of it ever happened. Because you've become too much a part of my life for me ever to let you go.*

Those were the things he wanted to say to her most of all.

He squeezed his hands into fists.

"Sean . . ."

"Don't," she told him.

Her voice was raw with emotion.

"We had an agreement," she said. "We promised ourselves we'd be sensible about this. I don't want some mushy good-byes spoiling it all."

He stared at her. "Is that what you think I'm doing? Trying to say good-bye?"

She just stared back at him.

"Isn't it?" she asked.

"No. *Hell*, no!"

He shook his head.

"Dammit, Sean, I'm trying to get you to change your mind."

She didn't say anything. She simply continued to stare at him.

"Look," he said. "I've heard all your reasons for why we shouldn't pursue anything long-term. You've got your career. Well, that's okay. I'd never want to stand in your way, and I'm willing to put my own career on hold for a while to give us a chance to make this work."

He raked his fingers through his wet hair again and paused for a breath, then continued before he lost his nerve again.

"I know that you have a problem becoming emotionally dependent on someone," he went on. "My telling you that it'll be okay and that I'll never leave you isn't going to matter. I know you're going to need time to figure that out for yourself, and I can live with that. I can give you all the time and space you need. I just . . ."

He took a deep breath. "I . . . just . . . need to know that you feel the same way about me that I do about you."

He held her gaze.

"I love you, Sean," he said quietly. "What I'm asking you is . . . do you love me?"

She swallowed.

"Yes."

She spoke so softly, he almost had to strain to catch her words.

"I love you."

TEN

For a long moment Sean stood there, staring at Dalton's face, hearing her voice echo over and over in her head like a piece of audiocassette caught in a continual loop.

I love you . . . I love you . . . I love you. . . .

She still couldn't believe that she'd said it. Lord knew that it wasn't what she had intended to say when he'd asked her the question. Not by a long damned shot. But when she'd opened her mouth to tell him that she was sorry, the other words had sort of tumbled from her lips in an automatic response. By the time she realized what she'd actually said, it had been much too late to censor herself.

Now . . . well, now she wouldn't dream

of censoring herself as a feeling of incredible inner peace descended over her.

It was, perhaps, the first real peace that she'd ever felt in her entire thirty years . . . just as having Dalton hold her close after they'd made love was the first real safety she'd ever known.

Her words had been true.

She loved him.

What's more, she knew in her heart—and in every fiber of her being—that he loved her too. She was probably more certain of those two simple truths than she was of anything else in the entire world.

"You do?" he asked her huskily. "You . . . love . . . me?"

She slowly nodded. "Yes. I love you."

The second time she said it was even easier than the first had been, so she tried for a third.

"I love you, Dalton."

He moved closer to her until only a heart-beat seemed to separate them.

"Then what the hell is the problem?" he asked, his voice going rough around the edges again. "If you love me . . . the way that I love you . . . then what have we been fighting about these past few weeks?"

"I wasn't aware that we'd been fighting," she said, trying to keep her own voice steady. "I told you the kind of relationship that I felt we could have, and you agreed to the terms.

You didn't even put up much resistance, as I recall."

"I had no choice," he told her. "It was either agree to an affair with you or lose you forever . . . and I'd have done almost anything to keep from losing you, sweetheart. Besides . . ."

He gave her a smile.

It was one of his better smiles, she decided. It was warm, full of caring . . . and filled with so much love that it nearly took her breath away.

"I figured that I would have plenty of time to try and change your mind about our not having a future together," he said.

"I see," she murmured.

"So have I?" he asked softly.

He reached for her hands, wrapped his long, warm fingers around her palms, and gave them a squeeze.

"Have I changed your mind about us?" he asked. "Or are you still maintaining that you're not interested in pursuing any kind of a long-term commitment?"

She took a deep breath. "Dalton, just because we love each other . . . well, it doesn't mean that things can necessarily work out between us."

He tugged on her hands, pulling her closer until their bodies touched. His clothes were as wet as hers, but the heat rising off his leanly muscular chest . . . combined with the heat of his smoke-filled gaze drilling into hers surrounded her, making her feel all warm and toasty inside.

"I realize that," he told her quietly. "And I'm not asking you for any guarantees."

Her heart started to pound. "That's good."

She knew only too well that life offered no real guarantees. Everything was a gamble, a calculated risk. The key was to choose those things that offered the most to gain . . . and the least to lose.

However, she still wasn't sure whether letting herself love Dalton was worth the risk.

"In fact," he went on, "I'm not asking you for anything that you can't give me openly and honestly. I love you, Sean. I want to spend the rest of my life loving you, holding you, kissing you."

A wave of panic swept over her. "Dalton . . ."

He smiled. "Sorry," he said, gently stroking her arms with his fingertips until the panic subsided. "I know I'm probably going a little too fast for you."

"You're going way too fast for me," she told him huskily. "I mean . . . you've got to give me a little time to adjust to all of this. I . . . I've never been in love before."

"It's okay," he told her. "Neither have I. Not like this anyway."

He released her arms, regarded her for a moment, then slid his palms under her chin and tilted her head up toward his.

"But this is right, Sean," he told her. "What we feel for each other . . . it was meant to be. Can't you sense that?"

"Yes," she murmured.

Being with Dalton had seemed so incredibly right from the first moment he'd kissed her, but changing the habits of a lifetime wasn't easy.

"And I don't want to hold back my feelings for you anymore," he said. "I love you, Sean, for now and for always . . . but I promised to give you as much time as you'll need to adjust to that, and I will. I'm here for keeps, sweetheart."

Then he gave her a slow, openmouthed kiss, the beauty and sensual power of which made her tremble. She wrapped her arms around his back and pulled him to her and just let herself feel the message he was sending her, soul to soul, heart to heart.

She felt the love and the caring and the goodness of him, and she drew it all in until it filled her, until it made the insecurities and the doubts seem far more trivial and far more manageable.

He kissed her until she was quite certain that, together, they could conquer anything.

Sometime later, she pulled back, feeling flushed and thoroughly kissed.

She gave him a smile.

"So what's this about putting your own career on hold for mine?" she asked, stroking her fingertips over his beard-stubbled chin.

"Hmm, that," he said.

"Yes, that. You know, it's not really necessary . . . unless, of course, you were referring to your taking the sabbatical from teaching to write that novel you told Sammy about?"

"That's exactly what I was referring to," he said, grinning at her. "Writing has been a dream of mine for a long time . . . ever since I was a child, it was all I wanted to do."

"It's the dream you had to abandon for things more practical when you grew up?" she asked, remembering their conversation out at the caverns.

She also remembered the regret she'd seen on his face as he'd talked about it.

"Yes," he told her. "Writing didn't seem to be very sensible or practical, so I told myself to forget about it and to pursue my second love, teaching. But then I met you. . . ."

He gently stroked his fingertips down the side of her cheek.

"You reminded me that dreams are something quite precious," he said.

"They are," she said huskily. "Because as long as you have your dreams, you can survive anything. And I think that you should pursue your dream of writing with every ounce of energy you have, but . . ."

He kept his gaze locked with hers. "But?" he repeated softly.

She took a deep breath. "But make sure you're pursuing it for the right reasons," she told him. "I don't want you to give up teaching for me. Dalton, you should want to take the sabbatical for yourself . . . for the chance it will give you to pursue your dream."

"I am, but you're so much a part of me, sweetheart, it would be impossible to separate the two. We need to spend time together, and we can't do that while I'm in Georgia and you're in Florida. Taking the sabbatical to write the book will give us that time."

"I know, but—"

"I want to do this," he said huskily. "But I'm going to need your support. After all, I may not have what it takes to be a writer. I could fail."

"It doesn't matter," she told him. "If you fail, you try again. Then again. You keep on trying until you finally succeed. After all, it's not the end result that is so important, remember? Sammy said it's the adventure. He was probably right . . . he's been right about a lot of things lately."

He grinned.

"Hmm," he murmured, pulling her to him again. "I've got a feeling that life with you is going to be one great adventure after another."

He slid his lips over hers again. The kiss was more tender this time, more seeped with sweet emotion.

Dalton was probably onto something there, she thought, pulling back to smile up at him.

Their life together would indeed be an adventure.

Perhaps the grandest adventure of all time.

Dalton decided that until Sean had murmured those three magical words, *I love you*, he had never known the true meaning of bliss. Or of joy. Or of ecstasy.

Now he did. They were all emotions that Sean had stirred to startling life inside him when she'd told him that she loved him. They were wonderful feelings too . . . feelings that only seemed to intensify each time he kissed her.

Perhaps that was why he loved kissing her so very much, he thought, smiling.

He tilted Sean's chin up so he could look at her. Their gazes locked.

There was no more pain in her eyes, he noticed with satisfaction. There was only love, so much love it made his heart rejoice.

"Speaking of adventures," he murmured huskily, stroking her jawline with the pad of his thumb, "what new ones do you see on our horizon? How many other pirates have you been dreaming about, sweetheart? Captain Kidd, maybe? Jean Laffite? Blackbeard? I'd like to know exactly what I'm in for here."

She laughed.

The husky sound wrapped itself around him as lovingly as an embrace.

"You're the only pirate I dream about these days," she said.

He felt his heart begin to swell. He loved her so much that he thought his heart would burst from all the joy and bliss and ecstasy she was releasing inside him.

He slid his hands around her waist. "So I'm the only pirate in your fantasies now?"

He hugged her to him, loving the damp smell of rain that clung to her hair almost as much as he did the faint floral scent of her perfume. He loved her.

And she loved him.

The realization still rocked him to his core.

"Yes," she murmured. "Especially in most of the wilder ones."

"Hmm. Well, I like the sound of that. Maybe you could tell me about a few of these wild pirate fantasies you've been having?"

She grinned. "You can count on it."

She skimmed her fingertips up his side, sending dozens of erotic tremors rocketing through him.

"Later, though," she added.

He brushed his lips over hers, his imagination already coming up with a few wild fantasies of his own.

"Fair enough," he said.

"But to answer your question about new expeditions," she said, "there really aren't any scheduled. The only jobs Setarip has lined up for the next few months are strictly marine salvage."

"No more treasure hunts?" he asked, feeling a little disappointed.

"No, but Ian has been talking about mounting a search for a cache of Confederate gold supposedly buried in Georgia. We may go forward with it next summer."

"Confederate gold, huh? Well, I'm ready whenever you are . . . once I pick up my laptop, I mean."

She laughed. "Oh, really?"

"Yes, really."

He paused a moment.

"I'd follow you anywhere, Sean," he said huskily.

Even to the depths of hell itself if he had to.

Dalton regarded her for a moment, then his expression grew serious.

"We are clear on what we're talking about here, aren't we?" he asked quietly. "I plan to move to Key Biscayne so we can continue our relationship to whatever final destination it may have. I'll have my own place, though. For now, we're going to take things slowly, but I want to build a future with you."

"I know," she said. Her voice was just as solemn as his. "But you don't have to rent your own apartment. You can live with me."

He thought about it. "Okay," he said. "As long as you realize that eventually, I'll want a more permanent commitment. I'll want marriage. Children."

"A whole passel of them?" she teased.

He grinned. "Why not?"

He pulled her to him, needing to feel her close.

"When I look at you," he whispered softly, "I see nothing but wonderful possibilities between us . . . and I'm willing to do whatever it takes to make those possibilities become realities."

She reached up and stroked his face. His heart started to pound.

"I see those same possibilities," she whispered back. "I see a family . . . our family . . . I can see it all when you touch me."

Then she wrapped her arms around his neck and pulled him closer. "I love you, Dalton. Somehow, I know this is all going to work out."

He hugged her back.

Somehow he knew it too.

THE EDITORS'
CORNER

Men. We love 'em, we hate 'em, but when it comes right down to it, we can't get along without 'em. Especially the ones we may never meet: those handsome guys with the come-hither eyes, those gentle giants with the hearts of gold, those debonair men who make you want to say yes. Well, this October you'll get your chance to meet those very men. Their stories make up LOVESWEPT's MEN OF LEGEND month. There's nothing like reuniting with an old flame, and the men our four authors have picked will definitely have you shivering with delight!

Marcia Evanick presents the final chapter in her White Lace & Promises trilogy, **HERE'S LOOKIN' AT YOU**, LOVESWEPT #854. Morgan De Witt promised his father that he would take care of his sister, Georgia. Now that Georgia's happily engaged, he's facing a lonely future and has decided it's time to find a Mrs. De Witt. Enter Maddie Andrews. Years ago, Maddie offered Morgan her heart, and he rebuffed the gawky fifteen-year-old. Morgan can't understand why Maddie is so aloof, but he's determined to crack her defenses, even if he has to send her the real Maltese Falcon to do so. Maddie's heart melts every time he throws in a line or two from her favorite actor, but can she overcome the fears bedeviling her every thought of happiness? As usual, Marcia Evanick delights readers with a love that is at times difficult, but always, always enduring.

Loveswept favorite Sandra Chastain returns with **MAC'S ANGELS: SCARLET LADY,** LOVESWEPT #855. Rhett Butler Montana runs his riverboat casino like the rogue he was named for, but when a mysterious woman in red breaks the bank and then dares him to play her for everything he owns, he's sorely tempted to abandon his Southern gentility in favor of a little one-on-one. With her brother missing and her family's plantation at stake, Katie Carithers has her own agenda in mind; she must form an uneasy alliance with the gambler who's bound by honor to help any damsel in distress. As the two battle over integrity, family, and loyalty, Katie and Rhett discover that what matters most is not material but intangible—that thing called love. Sandra Chastain ignites a fiery duel of wits and wishes when she sends a sexy rebel to do battle with his leading lady.

Next up is Stephanie Bancroft's delightful tale of Kat McKray and James Donovan, the former British agent who boasts a **LICENSE TO THRILL,** LOVESWEPT #856. Even though James Donovan is known the world over as untouchable and hard to hold, he has never lacked for companionship of the female persuasion. But after delivering a letter of historic consequence to the curvaceous museum curator, James is sure his sacred state of bachelorhood is doomed. Kat refuses to lose her heart to another love 'em and leave 'em kind of guy, a vow that slowly dissolves in the wake of James's presence. When Kat is arrested in the disappearance of the valuable artifact, it's up to James to save Kat's reputation and find the true culprit. In a romantic caper that taps into every woman's fantasy of 007 in hot pursuit, Stephanie keeps the pulse racing with a woman desperate to clear her name and that of the spy who loves her.

Talk about a tall tale! Donna Kauffman delivers **LIGHT MY FIRE**, LOVESWEPT #857, a novel about a smoke jumper and a maverick agent whose strength and determination are matched only by each other's. Larger than life, 6' 7" T. J. Delahaye rescues people for a living and enjoys it. By no means a shrinking violet at 6' 2", Jenna King rescues the environment and is haunted by it. But you know what they say—the bigger they are, the harder they fall—and these two are no exception. Trapped by the unrelenting forces of nature, Jenna and T. J. must rely on instinct and each other to survive. Sorrow has touched them both deeply, and if they make it through this ordeal alive, will they put aside the barriers long enough to learn the secret thrill of surrender? In a story fiercely erotic and deeply moving, Donna draws the reader into an inferno of emotion and fans the flames high with the heat of heartbreaking need.

Happy reading!

With warmest regards,

Susann Brailey   *Joy Abella*

Susann Brailey   Joy Abella

Senior Editor   Administrative Editor

P.S. Look for these Bantam women's fiction titles coming in October. From Jane Feather, Patricia Coughlin, Sharon & Tom Curtis, Elizabeth Elliott, Patricia Potter, and Suzanne Robinson comes **WHEN YOU WISH . . .** , a collection of truly romantic tales, in which a mysterious bottle containing one wish falls into the hands of each of the heroines . . . with magical results. Hailed by *Romantic Times* as "an exceptional talent with a tremendous gift for involving her readers in the story," Jane Ashford weaves a historical romance between Ariel Harding and the Honorable Alan Gresham, an unlikely alliance that will lead to the discovery of a dark truth and unexpected love in **THE BARGAIN**. National bestselling author Kay Hooper intertwines the lives of two women, strangers who are drawn together by one fatal moment, in **AFTER CAROLINE**. Critically acclaimed author Glenna McReynolds offers us **THE CHALICE AND THE BLADE**, the romantic fantasy of Ceridwen and Dain, struggling to escape the dangers and snares set by friend and foe alike, while discovering that neither can resist the love that promises to bind them forever. And immediately following this page, take a sneak peek at the Bantam women's fiction titles on sale in August.

Don't miss these extraordinary books
by your favorite Bantam authors!

On sale in August:

DARK PARADISE
by Tami Hoag

THE MERMAID
by Betina Krahn

BRIDE OF DANGER
by Katherine O'Neal

DARK PARADISE
by Tami Hoag

Here is nationally bestselling author Tami Hoag's breathtakingly sensual novel, a story filled with heart-stopping suspense and shocking passion . . . a story of a woman drawn to a man as hard and untamable as the land he loves, and to a town steeped in secrets—where a killer lurks.

She could hear the dogs in the distance, baying relentlessly. Pursuing relentlessly, as death pursues life.

Death.

Christ, she was going to die. The thought made her incredulous. Somehow, she had never really believed this moment would come. The idea had always loitered in the back of her mind that she would somehow be able to cheat the grim reaper, that she would be able to deal her way out of the inevitable. She had always been a gambler. Somehow, she had always managed to beat the odds. Her heart fluttered and her throat clenched at the idea that she would not beat them this time.

The whole notion of her own mortality stunned her, and she wanted to stop and stare at herself, as if she were having an out-of-body experience, as if this person running were someone she knew only in passing. But she couldn't stop. The sounds of the dogs drove her on. The instinct of self-preservation spurred her to keep her feet moving.

She lunged up the steady grade of the mountain, tripping over exposed roots and fallen branches. Brush grabbed her clothing and clawed her bloodied face like gnarled, bony fingers. The carpet of decay on the forest floor gave way in spots as she scrambled, yanking her back precious inches instead of giving her purchase to propel herself forward. Pain seared through her as her elbow cracked against a stone half buried in the soft loam. She picked herself up, cradling the arm against her body, and ran on.

Sobs of frustration and fear caught in her throat and choked her. Tears blurred what sight she had in the moon-silvered night. Her nose was broken and throbbing, forcing her to breathe through her mouth alone, and she tried to swallow the cool night air in great gulps. Her lungs were burning, as if every breath brought in a rush of acid instead of oxygen. The fire spread down her arms and legs, limbs that felt like leaden clubs as she pushed them to perform far beyond their capabilities.

I should have quit smoking. A ludicrous thought. It wasn't cigarettes that was going to kill her. In an isolated corner of her mind, where a strange calm resided, she saw herself stopping and sitting down on a fallen log for a final smoke. It would have been like those nights after aerobics class, when the first thing she had done outside the gym was light up. Nothing like that first smoke after a workout. She laughed, on the verge of hysteria, then sobbed, stumbled on.

The dogs were getting closer. They could smell the blood that ran from the deep cut the knife had made across her face.

There was no one to run to, no one to rescue her. She knew that. Ahead of her, the terrain only turned more rugged, steeper, wilder. There were no people, no roads. There was no hope.

Her heart broke with the certainty of that. No hope. Without hope, there was nothing. All the other systems began shutting down.

She broke from the woods and stumbled into a clearing. She couldn't run another step. Her head swam and pounded. Her legs wobbled beneath her, sending her lurching drunkenly into the open meadow. The commands her brain sent shorted out en route, then stopped firing altogether as her will crumbled.

Strangling on despair, on the taste of her own blood, she sank to her knees in the deep, soft grass and stared up at the huge, brilliant disk of the moon, realizing for the first time in her life how insignificant she was. She would die in this wilderness, with the scent of wildflowers in the air, and the world would go on without a pause. She was nothing, just another victim of another hunt. No one would even miss her. The sense of stark loneliness that thought sent through her numbed her to the bone.

No one would miss her.

No one would mourn her.

Her life meant nothing.

She could hear the crashing in the woods behind her. The sound of hoofbeats. The snorting of a horse. The dogs baying. Her heart pounding, ready to explode.

She never heard the shot.

FROM THE *New York Times* BESTSELLING

BETINA KRAHN

With the wit of *The Last Bachelor*, the charm of *The Perfect Mistress*, and the sparkle of *The Unlikely Angel*, Betina Krahn has penned an enchanting new romance

THE MERMAID

If Celeste Ashton hadn't needed money to save her grandmother's seaside estate, she would never have published her observations on ocean life and the dolphins she has befriended. So when her book makes her an instant celebrity, she is unprepared for the attention . . . especially when it comes from unnervingly handsome Titus Thorne. While Titus suspects there is something fishy about her theories, Celeste is determined to be taken seriously. Soon their fiery ideological clashes create sparks neither expects, and Titus must decide if he will risk his credibility, his career—and his heart—to side with the Lady Mermaid.

"KRAHN HAS A DELIGHTFUL, SMART TOUCH."
—*Publishers Weekly*

"Miss Ashton, permit me to apologize for what may appear to one outside the scientific community to be rudeness on the part of our members. We are all accustomed to the way the vigorous spirit of inquiry often leads to enthusiastic questioning and debate. The familiarity of long acquaintance and the dogged pursuit of truth sometimes lead us to overstep the bounds of general decorum."

She stared at the tall, dark-haired order bringer, uncertain whether to be irritated or grateful that he had just taken over her lecture.

"I believe I . . . understand."

Glancing about the lecture hall, she was indeed beginning to understand. She had received their invitation to speak as an honor, and had prepared her lecture under the assumption that she was being extended a coveted offer of membership in the societies. But, in fact, she had not been summoned here to *join;* she had been summoned here to *account.* They had issued her an invitation to an inquisition . . . for the grave offense of publishing research without the blessing of the holy orders of science: the royal societies.

"Perhaps if I restated a few of the questions I have heard put forward just now," he said, glancing at the members seated around him, "it would preserve order and make for a more productive exchange."

Despite his handsome smile and extreme mannerliness, her instincts warned that here was no ally.

"You state that most of your observations have been made while you were in the water with the creatures, themselves." As he spoke, he made his way to the end of the row, where the others in the aisle made way for him to approach the front of the stage.

"That is true," she said, noting uneasily the way the others parted for him.

"If I recall correctly, you stated that you sail or row out into the bay waters, rap out a signal on the hull of your boat, and the dolphin comes to greet you. You then slip into the water with the creature—or creatures, if he has brought his family group—hold your breath, and dive under the water to observe them."

"That is precisely what happens. Though I must say, it is a routine perfected by extreme patience and long experience. Years, in fact."

"You expect us to believe you not only call these creatures at will, but that you voluntarily . . . single-handedly . . . climb into frigid water with any number of these monstrous large beasts, and that you swim underwater for hours on end to observe them?" He straightened, glancing at the others as he readied his thrust. "That is a great deal indeed to believe on the word of a young woman who has no scientific training and no formal academic background."

His words struck hard and sank deep. So that was it. She was young and female and intolerably presumptuous to attempt to share her learning and experiences with the world when she hadn't the proper credentials.

"It is true that I have had no formal academic training. But I studied and worked with my grandfather for years; learning the tenants of reason and logic, developing theoretical approaches, observing and recording." She stepped out from behind the podium, facing him, facing them all for the sake of what she knew to be the truth.

"There is much learning, sir, to be had *outside* the hallowed, ivy-covered walls of a university. Experience is a most excellent tutor."

She saw him stiffen as her words found a mark in him. But a moment later, all trace of that fleeting reaction was gone.

"Very well, Miss Ashton, let us proceed and see what your particular brand of science has produced." His words were now tightly clipped, tailored for maximum impact. "You observe underwater, do you not? Just how do you *see* all of these marvels several yards beneath the murky surface?"

"Firstly, ocean water is not 'murky.' Anyone who has spent time at the seaside knows that." She moved to the table and picked up a pair of goggles. "Secondly, I wear these. They are known in sundry forms to divers on various continents."

"Very well, it might work. But several obstacles still remain. Air, for instance. How could you possibly stay under the water long enough to have seen all that you report?"

She looked up at him through fiercely narrowed eyes.

"I hold my breath."

"Indeed? Just how long can you hold your breath, Miss Ashton?"

"Minutes at a time."

"Oh?" His eyebrows rose. "And what proof do you have?"

"Proof? What proof do you need?" she demanded, her hands curling into fists at her sides. "Shall I stick my head in a bucket for you?"

Laughter skittered through their audience, only to die when he shot them a censuring look. "Perhaps we could arrange an impromptu test of your remarkable breathing ability, Miss Ashton. I propose that you hold your breath—right here, right now—and we will time you."

"Don't be ridiculous," she said, feeling crowded by his height and intensity. He stood head and shoulders above her and obviously knew how to use his size to advantage in a confrontation.

"It is anything *but* ridiculous," he declared. "It would be a demonstration of the repeatability of a phenomenon. Repetition of results is one of the key tests of scientific truth, is it not?"

"It would not be a true trial," she insisted, but loathe to mention why. His silence and smug look combined with derogatory comments from the audience to prod it from her. "I am wearing a 'dress improver,'" she said through clenched teeth, "which restricts my breathing."

"Oh. Well." He slid his gaze down to her waist, allowing it to linger there for a second too long. When she glared at him, he smiled. "We can adjust for that by giving you . . . say . . . ten seconds?"

Before she could protest, he called for a mirror to detect stray breath. None could be found on such short notice, so, undaunted, he volunteered to hold a strip of paper beneath her nose to detect any intake of air. The secretary, Sir Hillary, was drafted as a time-keeper and a moment later she was forced to purge her lungs, strain her corset to take in as much air as possible, and then hold it.

Her inquisitor leaned close, holding that fragile strip of paper, watching for the slightest flutter in it. And as she struggled to find the calm center into which she always retreated while diving, she began to feel the heat radiating from him . . . the warmth of his face near her own . . . the energy coming from his broad shoulders. And she saw his eyes, mere inches from hers, beginning to wander over her face. Was he purposefully trying to distract her? Her quickening pulse said that if he was, his tactic was working. To combat it, she searched desperately for someplace to fasten her vision, something to concentrate on. Unfortunately, the closest available thing was *him*.

Green eyes, she realized, with mild surprise. Blue

green, really. The color of sunlight streaming into the sea on a midsummer day. His skin was firm and lightly tanned . . . stretched taut over a broad forehead, high cheekbones, and a prominent, slightly aquiline nose. Her gaze drifted downward to his mouth . . . full, velvety looking, with a prominent dip in the center of his upper lip that made his mouth into an intriguing bow. There were crinkle lines at the corners of his eyes and a beard shadow was forming along the edge of his cheek.

She found herself licking her lip . . . lost in the bold angles and intriguing textures of his very male face . . . straining for control and oblivious to the fact that half of the audience was on its feet and moving toward the stage. She had never observed a man this close for this long—well, besides her grandfather and the brigadier. A man. A handsome man. His hair was a dark brown, not black, she thought desperately. And as her chest began to hurt, she fastened her gaze on his eyes and held on with everything in her. This was for science. This was for her dolphins. This was to teach those sea green eyes a lesson . . .

The ache in her chest gradually crowded everything but him and his eyes from her consciousness. Finally, when she felt the dimming at the edges of her vision, which spelled real danger, she blew out that breath and then gasped wildly. The fresh air was so intoxicating that she staggered.

A wave of astonishment greeted the news that she had held her breath for a full three minutes.

BRIDE OF DANGER
by Katherine O'Neal

Winner of the *Romantic Times* Award for Best
Sensual Historical Romance

*Night after night, she graced London's most elegant
soirees, her flame-haired beauty drawing all eyes, her
innocent charm wresting from men the secrets of their
souls. And not one suspected the truth: that she was a
spy, plucked from the squalor of Dublin's filthy streets.
For Mylene, devoted to the cause of freedom, it was a
role she gladly played . . . until the evening she came
face-to-face with the mysterious Lord Whitney. All of the
ton was abuzz with his recent arrival. But only Mylene
knew he was as much of an imposter as she. Gone was
any trace of Johnny, the wild Irish youth she
remembered. In his place was a rogue more devastatingly
handsome than any man had a right to be—and a rebel
coldheartedly determined to do whatever it took to fulfill
his mission. Now he was asking Mylene to betray
everything she'd come to believe in. And even as she
knew she had to stop him, she couldn't resist
surrendering to his searing passion.*

On the boat to England, Mylene had learned her role.
She was to play an English orphan who'd lost her
parents in an Irish uprising and, for want of any rela-
tions, had been shipped home to an English orphan-
age. The story would explain Mylene's knowledge of
Dublin. But more, it was calculated to stir the embers
of her adoptive father Lord Stanley's heart. He was
the staunchest opposition Parliament had to Irish
Home Rule. That Mylene's parents had been killed

by Irish rabble rousers garnered his instant sympathy. He'd taken her in at first glance, and formally adopted her within the year.

In the beginning, Mylene had been flabbergasted by her surroundings. She wasn't certain she could perform such an extended role without giving herself away. The luxurious lifestyle, the formalities and graces, proved matters of extreme discomfort. To be awakened in the warmth of her plush canopied bed with a cup of steaming cocoa embarrassed her as much as being waited on hand and foot. But soon enough, James—the driver who secretly worked for their cause—had passed along her assignment. She was to use her position to discover the scandalous secrets of Lord Stanley's friends and associates. Buoyed by the sense of purpose, she'd thrown herself into her task with relish, becoming accomplished at the subterfuge in no time.

What she hadn't counted on was growing to love Lord Stanley. Ireland, and her old life, began to seem like the dream.

"How fares the Countess?" he asked, thinking she'd gone to visit a friend.

"Well enough, I think, for all that her confinement makes her edgy."

"Well, it's all to a good purpose, as she'll see when the baby comes. But tell me, my dear, did her happy state have its effect? I shouldn't mind a grandchild of my own before too much time."

"The very thing we were discussing when you came in," announced his companion.

Mylene turned and looked at Roger Helmsley. He was a dashing gentleman of thirty years, tall with dark brown hair and a fetching pencil-thin mustache. He wore his evening clothes with negligent ease, secure in his wealth and position. He was Lord Stanley's compatriot in Parliament, the driving force behind the Irish opposition.

"Lord Helmsley has been pressing his suit," explained her father. "He informs me, with the most dejected of countenances, that he's asked for your hand on three separate occasions. Yet he says you stall him with pretty smiles."

"She's a coy one, my lord," said Roger, coming to take both her hands in his. "I daresay some of your own impeccable diplomacy has rubbed off on your daughter."

"Is this a conspiracy?" she laughed. "Is a girl not to be allowed her say?"

"If you'd say anything at all, I might bear up. But this blasted silence on the subject . . . Come, my sweet. What must an old bachelor like myself do to entice the heart of such a fair maiden?"

Roger was looking at her with a glow of appreciation that to this day made her flush with wonder. At twenty-two, Mylene had blossomed under the Earl's care. The rich food from his table had transformed the scrawny street urchin into a woman with enticing curves. Her breasts were full, her hips ripe and rounded, her legs nicely lean and defined from hours in the saddle and long walks through Hyde Park. Her skin, once so sallow, glowed with rosy health. Even her riotous curls glistened with rich abundance. Her pouty mouth was legendary among the swells of Marlboro House. Her clothes were fashioned by the best dressmakers in London, giving her a regal, polished air—if one didn't look too closely at the impish scattering of freckles across her nose. But when she looked in the mirror, she always gave a start of surprise. She thought of herself still as the ill-nourished orphan without so much as a last name.

It was partly this quest for a family of her own that had her considering Roger's proposal. He was an affable and decent man who, on their outings, had displayed a free-wheeling sense of the absurd that had brought an element of fun to her sadly serious life. His wealth, good looks, and charm were the talk of mothers with marriageable daughters. And if his politics appalled her, she'd learned long ago from Lord Stanley that a man could hold differing, even dangerous political views, and still be the kindest of men. Admittedly, the challenge intrigued her. As his wife, she could perhaps influence him to take a more liberal stance.

"You see how she avoids me," Roger complained in a melodramatic tone.

There was a knock on the door before the panels were slid open by Jensen, the all-too-proper major-domo who'd been in the service of Lord Stanley's grandfather. "Excuse the intrusion, my lord, but a gentleman caller awaits your pleasure without."

"A caller?" asked Lord Stanley. "At this hour?"

"His card, my lord."

Lord Stanley took the card. "Good gracious. Lord Whitney. Send him in, Jensen, by all means."

When Jensen left with a stiff bow, Roger asked, "A jest perhaps? A visit from the grave?"

"No, no, my good man. Not old Lord Whitney. It's his son. I'd heard on his father's death that he was on his way. Been in India with his mother since he was a lad. As you know, the climate agreed with her, and she refused to return when her husband's service was at an end. Kept the boy with her. We haven't seen the scamp since he was but a babe."

"Well, well, this *is* news! It's our duty, then, to set

him straight right from the start. Curry his favor, so to speak. We shouldn't want the influence he's inherited to go the wrong way."

"He's his father's son. He'll see our way of things, I'll warrant."

Mylene knew what this meant. Old Lord Whitney, while ill and with one foot in the grave, had nevertheless roused himself to Parliament in his wheelchair to lambaste, in his raspy voice, the MPs who favored Ireland's pleas. Lord Stanley, she knew, was counting on the son to take up the cause. It meant another evening of feeling her hackles rise as the gentlemen discussed new ways to squelch the Irish rebellion.

She kept her lashes lowered, cautioning herself to silence, as the gentleman stepped into the room and the doors were closed behind him.

Lord Stanley greeted him. "Lord Whitney, what a pleasant surprise. I'd planned to call on you myself, as soon as I'd heard you'd arrived. May I express my condolences for your father's passing. He was a distinguished gentleman, and a true friend. I assure you, he shall be missed by all."

Mylene felt the gentleman give a gracious bow.

"Allow me to present my good friend, Lord Helmsley. You'll be seeing a great deal of each other, I don't doubt."

The men shook hands.

"And this, sir, is my daughter, Mylene. Lord Whitney, from India."

Mylene set her face in courteous lines. But when she glanced up, the smile of welcome froze on her face.

It was Johnny!

On sale in September:

AFTER CAROLINE
by Kay Hooper

WHEN YOU WISH . . .
by Jane Feather, Patricia Coughlin, Sharon & Tom Curtis, Elizabeth Elliot, Patricia Potter, and Suzanne Robinson

THE BARGAIN
by Jane Ashford

THE CHALICE AND THE BLADE
by Glenna McReynolds

DON'T MISS THESE FABULOUS
BANTAM WOMEN'S FICTION TITLES

On Sale in August

DARK PARADISE
by TAMI HOAG,
The New York Times *bestselling author of* GUILTY AS SIN

A breathtakingly sensual novel filled with heart-stopping suspense and shocking passion . . . a story of a woman drawn to a man as hard and untamable as the land he loves, and to a town steeped in secrets—where a killer lurks. ____ 56161-8 $6.50/$8.99

THE MERMAID
by New York Times *bestseller* BETINA KRAHN,
author of THE UNLIKELY ANGEL

An enchanting new romance about a woman who works with dolphins in Victorian England and an academic who must decide if he will risk his career, credibility—and his heart—to side with the Lady Mermaid. ____ 57617-8 $5.99/$7.99

BRIDE OF DANGER
by KATHERINE O'NEAL,
winner of the Romantic Times *Award
for Best Sensual Historical Romance*

A spellbinding adventure about a beautiful spy who graces London's most elegant soirees and a devastatingly handsome rebel who asks her to betray everything she has come to believe in. ____ 57379-9 $5.99/$7.99

DON'T MISS THESE FABULOUS BANTAM WOMEN'S FICTION TITLES

On Sale in September

AFTER CAROLINE by Kay Hooper

A sensuous novel about the bewildering connection between two strangers who look enough alike to be twins. When one of them mysteriously dies, the survivor searches for the truth—was Caroline's death an accident, or was she the target of a killer willing to kill again?

___57184-2 $5.99/$7.99

WHEN YOU WISH...
by Jane Feather, Patricia Coughlin, Sharon & Tom Curtis, Elizabeth Elliott, Patricia Potter, and Suzanne Robinson

National bestseller Jane Feather leads a talent-packed line-up in this enchanting collection of six original—and utterly romantic—short stories. A mysterious bottle containing one wish falls into the hands of each of the heroines...with magical results.   ___57643-7 $5.99/$7.99

THE BARGAIN
by Jane Ashford, author of THE MARRIAGE WAGER

When a maddeningly forthright beauty and an arrogant, yet undeniably attractive scientist team up to rid London of a mysterious ghost, neither plans on the most confounding of all scientific occurrences: the breathless chemistry of desire.   ___57578-3 $5.99/$7.99

THE CHALICE AND THE BLADE
by Glenna McReynolds

In a novel of dark magic, stirring drama, and fierce passion, the daughter of a Druid priestess and a feared sorcerer unlock the mystery of an ancient legacy.   ___10384-9 $16.00/$22.95

Ask for these books at your local bookstore or use this page to order.

Please send me the books I have checked above. I am enclosing $_____ (add $2.50 to cover postage and handling). Send check or money order, no cash or C.O.D.'s, please.

Name _____

Address _____

City/State/Zip _____

Send order to: Bantam Books, Dept. FN158, 2451 S. Wolf Rd., Des Plaines, IL 60018
Allow four to six weeks for delivery.

Prices and availability subject to change without notice.   FN 158 9/97

Spellbinding, intoxicating, riveting...

Elizabeth Thornton's

gift for romance is nothing less than addictive

DANGEROUS TO LOVE

___56787-x $5.99/$7.99 Canada

DANGEROUS TO KISS

___57372-1 $5.99/$8.99 Canada

DANGEROUS TO HOLD

___57479-5 $5.99/$7.99 Canada

THE BRIDE'S BODYGUARD

___57425-6 $5.99/$7.99 Canada